"When we took our vows, we promised to love each other for better for worse," Philippe said slowly.

"We do! *I* do!"

"I never intended there to be a 'for worse' in our marriage." His voice grated. "This afternoon I had a visitor. It was a woman I rescued from an avalanche, months before I met you."

Kellie didn't need to hear another word to feel as if she'd been dropped from a high building.

"She must have had a good reason to visit a married man at the end of his workday." Kellie couldn't keep the tremor out of her voice.

"All I know is, she's eight months pregnant and claims it's my child."

Rebecca Winters, an American writer and mother of four, was excited about the new millennium because it meant another new beginning. Having said goodbye to the classroom where she taught French and Spanish, she is now free to spend more time with her family, to travel and to write the Harlequin Romance® novels she loves so dearly.

Readers are invited to visit Rebecca's Web site at www.rebeccawinters-author.com

Look out for *The Tycoon's Proposition*
by Rebecca Winters
on-sale December (#3729)

Books by Rebecca Winters

HARLEQUIN ROMANCE®

3693—THE BRIDEGROOM'S VOW
3703—HIS MAJESTY'S MARRIAGE (with Lucy Gordon)

THE BABY DILEMMA

Rebecca Winters

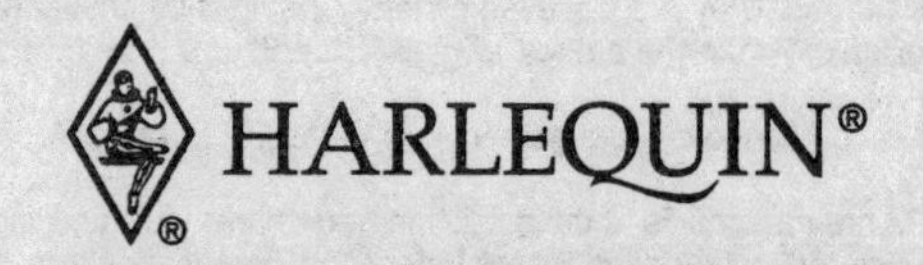

TORONTO • NEW YORK • LONDON
AMSTERDAM • PARIS • SYDNEY • HAMBURG
STOCKHOLM • ATHENS • TOKYO • MILAN • MADRID
PRAGUE • WARSAW • BUDAPEST • AUCKLAND

To Jo—someone who believed in my writing, cheered me on, let me explore to my heart's content and guided me to greater heights. I will always be grateful.

ISBN 0-373-03710-4

THE BABY DILEMMA

First North American Publication 2002.

This edition published by arrangement with Harlequin Books S.A.

Visit us at www.eHarlequin.com

Printed in U.S.A.

CHAPTER ONE

September 29

To My Darling Philippe—

In honor of that unforgettable moment in the meadow below Mount Rainier when you proposed to me.

These gold cuff links contain the tiniest petals of the wildflowers you gathered for me. They're very precious because they represent your love. No woman ever felt more loved by her husband than I do. Happy one month anniversary, sweetheart.

Kellie

Putting her pen aside, Kellie Madsen Didier slid the card inside the envelope and taped it to the present she'd wrapped in black with red, green and gold foil ribbon. It had required painstaking work to arrange the petals in a design which would fit beneath the oval glass overlays trimmed in gold. But the result had pleased her.

Philippe would be walking through the door of their elegant Neuchâtel penthouse apartment any second. The windows gave out on a magnificent view of Lake Neuchâtel, one of Switzerland's most beautiful scenic sights. Truly he'd brought her home to paradise.

She hurried out of the bedroom to the living room where she'd wheeled in the tea cart for a special dinner.

It was set with their best lace cloth, china, crystal and silver. In the cut crystal vase she'd placed a bouquet of fall flowers backed by an ornate candelabra. She put his gift next to his goblet, then rushed to the kitchen to finish up last minute preparations.

As soon as he'd left for the office that morning, she'd laid her French studies aside to work on a fabulous gourmet meal. After cooking and cleaning most of the day, she'd stopped long enough to shower and wash her hair.

Now that it was dry, it fell over one shoulder, partially hiding the capped sleeve of her new figure-hugging black crepe dress. Philippe had often remarked that with her green eyes and long caramel hair streaked by natural blond highlights, she looked stunning in black.

Wearing dainty black high heels to add a few inches to her five-foot-six frame, she hoped to dazzle him all over again tonight.

She glanced at her watch. Seven-thirty. He was almost a half hour later than he said he'd be when he'd called her that afternoon. It wasn't like him not to phone again if he'd been detained by a client.

Earlier in the week he'd told her the ambassador from *La Côte D'Ivoire* had been in to order a fleet of limousines. Maybe there'd been a glitch during shipment from the Didier luxury automanufacturing plant in Paris.

Philippe could still be in the process of ironing out any number of problems. He was meticulous about his work. However until she heard his key in the lock, she didn't want to light the candles.

Kellie went back to the kitchen to check on everything. Ten minutes slipped by, then another ten. Starting to get worried, she rang him on his cell phone, but she reached his voice mail asking the caller to leave a message.

Growing more anxious she phoned his personal secretary, Marcel, at home. The other man told her he'd last seen Philippe at his desk talking long distance to New York when they'd waved good-night to each other.

Marcel suggested her husband might be discussing something with the night security guard or the custodial staff before he left the showroom office. He urged her not to become alarmed. There could be a dozen reasons why he was late. Perhaps he was entertaining a businessman.

She thanked Marcel and hung up, but she was not reassured. Philippe would have asked her to join him if he'd planned to take a buyer out to dinner.

One of his good friends and climbing buddies, Roger, had dropped by night before last. Was it possible he hadn't gone back to Zermatt and was still in Neuchâtel? When they got talking about their favorite subject, they forgot anyone else was in the room.

She ran to the study to look up Roger's number. Before she could find it on the card Philippe kept at the side of his desk, the phone rang.

Pouncing on the receiver, she put it to her ear. "Hello?"

"Madame Didier?" came a serious sounding voice.

A sense of foreboding set her on the verge of panic. Her mouth went dry. "Yes? This is she."

"I'm calling from the emergency room at Vaudois Hospital. Your husband is going to be fine, but he was in an automobile accident and is asking for you."

Oh Dear God.

"I'll be right there!" she cried.

After hanging up, she rang for a taxi.

Kellie could have taken the new little sports car Philippe had bought her for a wedding present. It was sitting in the apartment garage. But she didn't know the location of the hospital, and didn't want to worry about finding a place to park. In truth, she was shaking so hard she didn't know if she'd be able to drive.

Another dash through the rooms to get her purse and turn off the oven, then she left the apartment on a run. Too impatient to wait for the lift, she hurried down the four flights of stairs to the main floor in her high heels and rushed outside, oblivious to the nip in the air.

When she saw a taxi turn the corner, she ran out to the street and waved him down. After climbing in she said, "The Vaudois Hospital, please, *monsieur.*"

"Oui, madame."

She hugged her arms to her waist anxiously. If he'd sustained serious injuries, the person on the phone wouldn't have said Philippe was all right. Still, she wouldn't be able to breathe normally again until she could hold him and see him with her own eyes.

"Please hurry. My husband has been in an accident. Let me off at the entrance to the emergency room," she said in French to the driver. He nodded, but didn't accelerate that much through the moderate nighttime traffic. Switzerland was a very dignified, civilized country with few drivers who took dangerous risks.

She couldn't say the same for Philippe who was French born. According to his family with whom she'd lived for a month near the Bois de Vincennes in Paris, he'd been a daredevil from birth.

Apparently he'd raced cars in his early twenties and drove at speeds that terrified most people. His sister,

Claudine, Kellie's dear friend, had confided that though he may have abandoned that pleasure once he'd discovered his great love for mountain climbing, he could still let it rip once in a while testing out one of the new sports models fresh from the plant. If that's what he'd done tonight, then it was too high a price to pay.

When she thought she couldn't stand it any longer, they reached the hospital where she could see several ambulances outside the doors. The sight of them enlarged the pit in her stomach.

"We're here, *madame.*"

"*Merci, monsieur.*" She climbed out of the taxi, handing him several bills of Swiss francs without bothering to count how much she'd given him. Then she raced inside the entrance.

The reception room was packed with friends and family of casualty victims talking quietly. Their anxiety-ridden faces revealed their stress. As she approached the woman at the desk, Kellie happened to see herself in the glass and knew her expression was no different.

"Excuse me. I'm Madame Didier. My husband, Philippe, was brought in tonight. Where can I find him?"

"Through there on the left. He's been put in cubicle four."

"Thank you," Kellie whispered before hurrying through the swinging doors to the E.R. Again she was struck by the amount of activity going on. Medical staff, paramedics, even police came and went from the busy room. It looked as if every cubicle was in use. Behind the curtain of the first one she could hear a woman wailing in pain.

Full of gratitude it wasn't Philippe in that kind of agony, she ran to number four and parted the curtain to reach her husband. He was awake, thank heaven! She flew to his side where he lay in a hospital gown beneath a pristine white sheet.

"Philippe?"

"*Mon amour*— I thought you'd never get here."

His deep voice sounded so shaken, it astounded her. Philippe was the kind of man whose intelligence and strong personality inspired confidence in everyone around him. Not only physically powerful, he exuded an inner male strength and drive that made him seem invincible.

"I came the second they phoned me, darling," she cried, utterly thrown by his vulnerability. "I've been home waiting hours for you to arrive."

Beneath his beautiful olive skin there was an unnatural pallor, but the devilishly handsome face with those black-brown eyes and black hair she loved was still the same.

"*Mon Dieu.* You're so beautiful, it hurts." In a swift motion he lifted his right arm to draw her head down, but she noticed he didn't try to use his left one at all. She was so preoccupied about that, she wasn't prepared for his kiss which was almost savage in its intensity.

Since they'd been married, they'd made love day and night, under every circumstance and condition. But her husband had never embraced her as if it were going to be their last.

"Philippe, sweetheart—" she whispered after he'd unwillingly relinquished her lips. "I can tell your left arm is hurt."

"My elbow got banged. It's nothing."

Her anxious eyes played over him. "What else is wrong with you?"

"A bump on my left kneecap."

"Oh, darling," she moaned. "Let me see."

"There's no need. From what the doctor told me, neither is broken, just bruised. They'll take some X rays in a while to be certain. I'm waiting my turn. Before they come for me, there's something we have to talk about."

Again she felt this sense of foreboding. After taking a shuddering breath she said, "All right."

She heard him invoke God's help before he murmured, "Maybe you'd better sit down."

With those fateful words, Kellie needed support. She saw a stool by the shelving and moved it next to the bed where she could prop herself. Grasping his right hand which she kissed and held to her cheek she said, "What's this terrible thing you have to tell me?"

His expression grew bleak before his eyes filled with pleading.

"Sweetheart?" she begged, unable to stand the suspense another second.

He cleared his throat. "When we took our vows, we promised to love each other for better or worse."

"We do! *I* do!"

"I never intended for there to be a 'for worse' in our marriage," his voice grated.

"But there is?" She swallowed hard.

"Kellie, I don't know how to say this."

"Say what?" she demanded in agony, freeing her hand to run her fingers through his dark wavy hair. "Don't you know you can tell me anything?"

His eyes looked haunted. "Late this afternoon while I was finishing up some work at the office so I could get home to you, I had a visitor. It was a woman I rescued after an avalanche in Chamonix months before I met you."

Kellie didn't need to hear another word to feel as if she'd been dropped from a high building.

"Her name's Yvette Boiteux."

It didn't sound familiar. According to Claudine, until Kellie had come along, her brother had left a trail of broken hearts that stretched from Paris to Neuchâtel.

"She must have had a good reason to visit a married man at the end of his workday." Kellie couldn't keep the tremor out of her voice.

"All I know is, she's eight months pregnant and claims it's my child."

Kellie bit down so hard on her knuckle, it drew blood.

"Darling—" He gripped her free hand tightly, not knowing his strength. "Please hear me out."

She averted her eyes. "I'm listening."

"We only slept together once, and I took precautions. It was a mistake from start to finish. I realize my reputation precedes me, but in reality, there've only been a few women. Yvette wasn't one of them."

It was hard to breathe. "I believe you."

By now he was gripping her hand so hard, it hurt. But she invited it to counteract this other pain which had penetrated the core of her being where there could be no earthly relief.

"When she came to my office, she didn't look well to me. She told me she'd come by bus because she didn't own a car. At that point I told her I'd drive her home.

"Before I said anything about having a paternity test done, I was praying she would admit that one of her lovers had turned his back on her. Knowing I was good for the money, it would explain the reason why she'd come to me at the midnight hour for financial help."

Kellie's eyes closed tightly for a moment. *What if the test came up with a match?*

"On the way to the apartment where she told me she lived with her mother, a tourist ran into us. He received the citation for driving out of control. Under other circumstances I might have been able to see him coming to avoid a collision."

She shook her head. "After news like that, I don't know how you could even function."

He let out a tortured sound. "As it happens, the impact shoved my car against a parked van. The doctor said Yvette doesn't have any injuries, but at this stage of her pregnancy, the shock could bri—"

"Monsieur Didier?" an unfamiliar voice broke in on them. "We're ready to take you to X ray. Madame—If you wouldn't mind stepping out for a moment, our team will get him transferred to the gurney," the technician said to Kellie.

"Yes, of course."

"Darling—" Philippe's voice sounded frantic.

"I'll be right outside the curtain."

She pushed the stool back in place, then lifted the flap to wait in the main room of the E.R. In a minute the technicians emerged with Philippe. Like lasers, his dark eyes burned into her soul.

"Promise me you'll be here when I get back."

The tears she'd been fighting spilled down her cheeks. "Where would I go?"

You're my whole life, Philippe. Without you, there's nothing.

When he'd disappeared through another set of doors, she realized his parents needed to be notified, then Marcel. But her body was slow to obey her brain.

As she retraced her steps to the reception area to

make the calls, she heard the hysterical woman behind the first curtain crying out Philippe's name. Kellie froze.

"Calm yourself, Mademoiselle Boiteux," said another female voice. "Monsieur Didier will be in to visit you as soon as he comes back from X ray."

"I need to see him. I love him. He's the father of my baby. I'm going to have his son. Promise me he's not hurt, that he's all right!"

"You mustn't get upset. It isn't good for you or the baby. You have toxemia. Your blood pressure's too high. We need to get it down, so you have to cooperate with us."

"It was my fault we were in the accident. He offered to drive me home and I let him. I shouldn't have agreed to it, then he wouldn't have been hurt. He's so wonderful. He saved my life once before. If anything happened to Philippe, I'd want to die."

"No, *mademoiselle.* You want to live. You're going to be a mother very soon. Think of the joy you'll have in raising your child. We've called your mother. She'll be here soon to comfort you."

"No," she cried out. "Without Philippe, I don't care about anything else. Please tell him to come. This is his child. You don't understand. He's my whole life!"

This is his child. He's my whole life.

Kellie felt as if someone had just walked across her grave.

A hand touched her shoulder. "Madame? You look like you're feeling ill," one of the nurse's aides observed. "Do you want to lie down?"

"N-no. I'll be all right."

"Let me at least help you to the reception room where you can sit while you wait for your husband."

"Thank you."

Her limbs felt wooden as he assisted her to a chair beyond the swinging doors.

"Someone will let you know when he's been brought back. Is there anything I can do for you?"

Kellie felt like she was in the middle of a nightmare where she was running from something, but everything was happening in slow motion.

"Could you please phone his secretary and inform him of the accident? He lives here in town. Ask him to call Philippe's parents." She would phone everyone later, but for the moment her strength seemed to have left her body.

He pulled a notepad out of his pocket. "What's the secretary's name and number?"

She gave the aide the information. Once he'd disappeared, she sat there until her terrible weakness had passed. Then she got up from the chair and went over to the woman at the desk.

"Would you call me a taxi please."

Ten minutes later, Kellie entered the apartment. She walked straight into Philippe's study and sat down at his desk. Withdrawing the gold pen from its holder, one of their many wedding gifts, she reached for a notepad.

My darling husband—

Never doubt that I will always love you, but Yvette loved you first. We've only been married thirty days. She's been carrying your baby for eight months. The "for worse" part of our vows didn't cover that.

I heard her call out your name. She had no idea I could follow her conversation with the doctor from the outside of the curtain. She was begging, pleading for you to come to her.

After the things she told the doctor in confidence,

there's no doubt Yvette is pregnant with your son. I don't blame you for anything, darling. But you must see she needs your help and protection now because she's very sick with a high-risk pregnancy.

I know you're not the kind of man to abandon your responsibilities the way my birth father abandoned my mother and me, so I'm going back to Washington. When I get there, I'll start divorce proceedings. Soon you'll be free to marry her and be a full-time father to your child.

Be assured the only alimony I want is your promise that you'll do the right thing for Yvette and your son. No one will make a better father than you.

All my love, Kellie.

She pulled off her wedding ring and left it on top of the note, then she phoned for another taxi to drive her to the airport. She'd worry about what plane to take when she got there.

Before the taxi arrived, she changed into wool pants and a sweater. After putting the food in the fridge and straightening the kitchen, she threw some clothes and toiletries in an overnight bag. When her packing was done, she grabbed her passport out of the dresser drawer, left her car keys on top, then walked out of the apartment without looking back.

The second she got into the taxi, her cell phone rang. She ignored it and told the chauffeur to get her to Geneva as quickly as possible.

During the drive, the phone went off at least twenty different times. Evidently Philippe had come back from X ray and was wondering where she'd gone.

The ringing would stop once the doctors told him

Yvette was calling for him and he realized how sick she was.

"Kellie?" Her grandfather's gray head peered around the door of the restaurant's kitchen. "The phone's for you!"

"I'll have to call them back, grandpa."

He walked behind the huge stainless-steel island where she was preparing the salads. "It's Claudine."

Fresh pain stabbed her heart.

"You've avoided every call from Philippe since you got home a week ago. Surely you're not going to ignore his sister, too. That's not right, honey. I'll take over here. You go upstairs to the office and talk to her."

She took a deep breath, realizing this couldn't be put off any longer. In any event, it wasn't fair to her family.

"All right. I won't be long."

"Take all the time you need. You're so bottled up, you're going to explode one of these days. It'll do you good to talk to her. She's a sweetie."

Kellie's grandfather, James Madsen, was crazy about Claudine who had lived with them for a month during her American homestay. She was a Didier through and through. Dark good looks, intelligent, high class, charm galore.

He loved talking fractured French to her, and was hurt because Kellie's marriage to her brother had broken up. Everyone in her family knew the reason why she was getting a divorce. She loved them for never having said a negative word or interfering.

But she was aware that they were very fond of Philippe. Kellie's mom was still grieving over her daughter's smashed dreams, yet they'd all honored her wishes by keeping silent.

She hurried to the sink to wash her hands. After leaving the kitchen she raced up the stairs to the next floor where their family lived above the thriving restaurant.

Her grandfather had bought the property and opened it in the late sixties. He'd named it The Eatery, a play on words because they lived in Eatonville, Washington, gateway to the Cascades and Mount Rainier.

Growing up it had been Kellie's dream to turn it into a French restaurant one day. All her university education in French, plus her subsequent training as a French chef in Napa Valley, California, had been chosen with that end in mind.

Then her grandfather had surprised her by sending her to France on a homestay through the university to improve her French. That was how she'd met Claudine. It was there in the Didier home she'd been introduced to Philippe who just happened to be visiting his family for the day.

One look at him and she'd fallen so deeply in love, her entire world had changed. Evidently it had for him, too, because when the homestay came to an end, he'd followed her back to Washington. Before the month was out they'd celebrated their wedding.

After experiencing euphoria in her thirty-day marriage to him, she realized life would never hold that same magic for her again. Not ever.

She'd been trying so hard to put the past behind her. But she knew the second she heard his sister's voice, the pain was going to come crashing through.

Her hand trembled as she picked up the receiver in her grandfather's study. "Hello, C-Claudine?"

"Kellie—" her friend let out a mournful cry. "At last."

She could hardly swallow, let alone talk. "I—I'm sorry it has taken me so long to face you."

"Don't apologize, *chérie.* I love Philippe, too, and cry myself to sleep every night for what has happened."

"H-how is he?"

"If you mean physically, he's recovering. The bone on his elbow was bruised, but he no longer has to wear a sling. His knee required surgery. Otherwise he would have come after you."

A quiet gasp escaped Kellie's throat. His injuries had been worse than he'd made out. Who had been taking care of him?

"Now he's on crutches to keep the weight off it until it's healed."

Every word from Claudine's lips tore her apart a little more.

"Kellie—you have to know that mentally my brother's devastated you left him," she confided in a tremulous voice.

By now the tears were dripping off her cheeks. "Did he ask you to call me?"

"No. He isn't talking to anyone about anything. His pain is too deep. I've been praying you might have had time to reconsider your decision."

"It's all I think about." She half-sobbed. "But no matter how I view it, divorce is the only answer. Cutting ties with me frees him to fulfill his moral obligation. You and I both know what kind of a father he'll make. You've seen him interact with your nieces and nephew. It's one of the qualities about him that made me want to marry him."

"My brother can be a model father without marrying her!"

"Visitation isn't the same thing as belonging to one

family. He mustn't deprive Yvette's baby of its father. I had to live my whole life without mine, and I don't want his son to know the same deprivation. Not only that, Philippe has wanted to get started on a family. Well, now he has one... Yvette adores him, and their child will be born any day now.''

''That's not the point, Kellie. He's too deeply in love with you to consider marriage to anyone else.''

''But there was a time when he cared for Yvette. Given a chance, those feelings could turn into love. He's going to worship his child. If you were in my shoes, would you deny him the chance to raise their infant in his own household with the baby's birth mother?''

A brief silence ensued. ''I can't answer that. I don't know what it's like to grow up without a father. Obviously it has scarred you much more than I'd realized.''

''Claudine— I heard Yvette confide in the doctor at the hospital right after they'd brought her in. The pain and the longing in her voice for Philippe killed me. I knew then what I had to do.''

Again there was a hesitation before Claudine said, ''What about *your* pain and longing for my brother?''

''It doesn't matter about me.''

''That's what you say now. But there's going to come a day... I hope you won't live to regret it.''

''Please don't hate me, Claudine,'' she begged.

''I won't dignify your comment with a response. As for Philippe, I'm sure he wishes he could hate you. It would make things easier all the way around. Have you been to an attorney yet?''

She sucked in her breath. ''Yes. Philippe will be receiving the papers next week.''

"It's going to kill him."

"Don't say that."

"I *have* to say it because I know my brother. You think a divorce will force him to marry Yvette, but you're wrong. He loves *you.* Our whole family loves you."

"I love all of you, too," her voice trembled. "I love you for caring so much, but Yvette and her baby are the important ones here."

There was a pause. "Kellie?"

She wiped her eyes with the back of her free hand. "Yes?"

"You're the only wife he wants."

"He'll change his mind when he's there for the delivery and lays eyes on his little lookalike for the first time."

"I think you're wrong."

"Claudine—"

"I'm sorry. I promised myself I wouldn't put pressure on you, and that's all I've done since I rang."

"You have no reason to apologize. I'm so awful I haven't even asked how things are going with Jules."

"They're not."

"Why?"

"Unlike my brother, I think he's a *real* playboy who'll never settle down. He's too attractive, has too much money. He can put on a convincing act that I'm the only woman for him, but I know deep down that's not true.

"One day he'll get bored and move on. I feel it in my bones. He doesn't know it yet, but I've had my last date with him. I've got to keep looking for Mr. Perfect. Unfortunately no one ever measures up to Philippe."

It always came down to Philippe.

No one could compare to him, but Kellie did know one man who had many of her husband's sterling qualities. It was his good friend, Roger. Ever since she'd met him, she'd thought he and Claudine might hit it off. It was a subject she'd intended to broach with her husband.

Now there was no more Philippe. At least not in her world.

"I can tell you want to hang up, Kellie. Please call me once in a while. I couldn't take it if you cut me off, too."

"I would never do that. You'll hear from me soon. I swear it."

"A tout à l'heure, chérie."

"À bientôt, chère Claudine."

Kellie hung up the phone, dissolved in fresh tears.

Unable to bear the pain, she ran through the house to her room and collapsed on the bed.

CHAPTER TWO

KELLIE?''

Her head swerved toward the nurse. ''Yes?''

''Dr. Evans wants to talk to you. As soon as you're dressed, just step into his office.''

''All right.''

Dr. Evans had been the Madsen family doctor for as long as she could remember. He'd seen her through everything from tonsils and stitches to fractures and flu.

Lately she'd been having headaches and could pinpoint the onset of them to the day Kellie's attorney had sent Philippe's solicitor the divorce papers by express mail. The packet had gone out a week ago. Since then, the calls from Philippe had stopped.

It was what she'd wanted, but she couldn't help but be anxious about him and needed to know if the baby had been born yet. She could always phone Claudine. However a part of her was afraid that if she did that, she'd break down crying again and it would make her headaches worse.

Hopefully Kellie's doctor could prescribe something to take them away. The normal over-the-counter drugs weren't helping.

A few minutes later she left the examining room and walked into his office. He was waiting for her. ''Sit down, Kellie.''

After she'd taken a seat opposite his desk he smiled at her. ''I believe I've discovered the source of your headaches, but I'll leave it up to your obstetrician for a final determination."

Kellie blinked. *Obstetrician?*

He stared at her. "You didn't have any idea you were pregnant?"

She lurched in the chair. If she hadn't been holding on to the sides, she might have fallen out of it.

His expression grew solemn. "I take it you and your husband hadn't planned on starting a family yet."

"No— I—I mean we *did* want a baby. But we c-can't have one now. We just can't!" she cried in anguish.

He leaned toward her, looking at her in that confiding way. "Kellie? In twenty-five years I've never seen you this emotional. Obviously something traumatic is going on in your life, thus the reason for the headaches."

His confiding tone had the effect of opening the dam. She buried her face in her hands and sobbed.

He passed her the box of tissues on his desk. "Tell me what's wrong."

Dr. Evans had always been like a father confessor, but for the first time in her life, she found she couldn't talk to him. Not about this.

How could she explain her feelings over finding out she was pregnant with Philippe's child when he was awaiting the birth of his son right now? Maybe Yvette had already delivered.

"I'm sorry," she said a few minutes later, lifting her head to wipe her eyes. "Please forgive my outburst. Thank you for seeing me, but right now I'm afraid I have to go." She shot out of the chair.

His concerned gaze followed her to the door. "I'm the one who's sorry. In light of your pregnancy, promise me you'll get hold of an OB right away. Dr. Cutler's one of the best. His office is on the second floor. Tell him I referred you."

She nodded. "Thank you, Dr. Evans."

"You want to have a healthy child. Don't wait too long to start your prenatal care, and don't take any medication unless you've cleared it with your OB first!"

"I won't. Goodbye."

Kellie couldn't get out of his office fast enough.

She hurried down to the car park and drove back to the café. It opened for lunch in half an hour. She needed to get busy going over the dinner menu.

Her family didn't know she'd been to the doctor. Until she'd made a decision about what to do, she didn't want to tell them what she'd learned. At the moment she was still trying to absorb the news with all its ramifications.

In order to avoid conversation, she parked behind the restaurant and slipped in the rear entrance which was used for delivery people. Luckily the other chef and the serving help were working at a steady pace. There was no unnecessary talk, especially on Fridays which brought in the large weekend crowds of tourists on their way to and from the Cascades.

Her grandparents did the cashiering while her mom ran the dining room. That left Kellie in the kitchen to hide her grief over an untenable situation. But by four o'clock that afternoon her head was splitting.

She told the other chef she needed to quit for the day. Excusing herself, she went up to her room and called Dr. Cutler's office for an appointment. The receptionist fit her in for the following Friday.

When Kellie explained about her headaches, the nurse came on the line and told her of one painkiller she could take that wouldn't hurt the baby.

Kellie thanked her for the information and hung up. She'd already tried it, but she'd received no relief. The only thing to do was go to bed and hope she could sleep it off.

To some degree her solution worked. A short nap seemed to stave off the worst of the pain.

Over the next seven days while she waited to find out if Philippe's solicitor had responded, she would excuse herself to lie down as soon as she felt a headache coming on.

After her appointment with Dr. Cutler on Friday, Kellie made the decision to tell her family about her condition. As soon as they closed the restaurant for the night, she would sit down with them.

"Kellie?"

"What is it, Roy?" she asked the college age waiter who'd come in the kitchen for the steak dinners she'd put under the warmer.

"Someone's out in front wanting to speak to you. The woman said she'd wait until you had a break."

"I've already had mine for today. Who is it?"

"I don't know. I've never seen her before or believe me, I would have remembered." He smiled. "It was Lee something. Her last name started with an *M,* but I can't pronounce it."

Kellie didn't know a woman named...wait a minute— No. It couldn't be *that* Lee, the wife of Philippe's best friend, Raoul.

While Kellie had lived in the apartment with Philippe, Prince Raoul Mertier Bergeret D'Arillac, ruler of the French-Swiss cantons and his new twenty-six-year old American bride who was the same age as Kellie, had still been out of the country on their honeymoon.

Though Kellie had never met either of them, she'd seen the news clippings of their royal wedding among the things in Philippe's desk. He also had hundreds of photos and various videos of Raoul and his friends out climbing.

If the prince and his wife had taken up residence in Neuchâtel since Kellie's flight from Switzerland, they couldn't possibly be here. *Could they?*

"Hey— Kellie— What do you want me to say?"

His question brought her thoughts back to the present. "Roy—did her last name sound like Mertier?"

He nodded. "That's it exactly!"

Kellie's legs started to shake.

If Lee Mertier of all people was in The Eatery dining room, then the only reason she would be here was that something terrible had happened to Philippe. Maybe his injuries were worse than Claudine had made them out to be.

"Tell her to meet me in the foyer. I'll be right there."

"Okay."

As soon as he left the kitchen with the dinners, Kellie told the other chef she needed more time off. After washing her hands in the sink, she hung her apron and hair net on a peg in the back room. On trembling legs she made her way through the kitchen and dining room to the restaurant lobby.

The reality of the lovely, vital woman with short silvery-gold hair and violet eyes who turned in Kellie's direction surpassed her image of the princess in the newspaper photos. Yet in jeans and a knit top, Lee Mertier looked completely down to earth and approachable.

As Kellie hurried past a line of customers to reach

the other woman, she was so terrified to hear bad news about Philippe, she could hardly breathe.

"Princess?" she said in a shaky voice.

"Call me Lee." She flashed her a sweet smile. "I knew you had to be Kellie. You're more beautiful than the picture Philippe carries around with him."

"Maybe he did once," she said in a tortured whisper. "I was about to tell you no news clipping could do you justice."

"Thank you."

"Please—" Kellie struggled to keep her emotions under control. "I know you wouldn't be here if something weren't seriously wrong with Philippe. Were his injuries from the car accident more severe than his sister led me to believe?"

Shadows darkened Lee's eyes, increasing Kellie's fears. "He's not dying, so let me put your mind at rest about that."

"Is there something wrong with the baby?"

"Kellie?" she said quietly. "Can we go someplace to be alone and talk?"

"Yes. Of course. Forgive my lack of manners. I—I admit I'm scared to death."

Kellie opened the door to the stairway, urging Lee to follow her up to the living room of the house.

"Please sit down. Can I get you anything?"

"No, thank you." She found a place on the end of the couch. Kellie took a chair opposite her.

The other woman spoke first. "I know my presence has alarmed you, but after discussing it with Raoul, we agreed this wouldn't work over the phone."

"Did your husband come with you?"

"No. I left him hosting an international bankers' conference he'd already put off once before."

"But you're barely home from your honeymoon, aren't you? To think you had to leave him to fly this far—"

"My husband loves Philippe like a brother. He'd do anything for him. I'm pretty crazy about your husband myself. The problem is, he's not the same man who introduced me to Raoul in Zermatt. All traces of the dashing Frenchman who lost his heart to you have vanished."

Kellie's head was bowed.

"He's in such a severe emotional crisis right now, my husband I are deeply concerned."

"I'm sure that being a new father, plus trying to help Yvette with their little boy must be—"

"Kellie—" Lee interrupted. "Yvette died during the delivery."

"What?" she cried out aghast, unable to remain seated. Claudine hadn't phoned to let her know. "I thought Philippe said she wasn't injured in the car accident."

"Just listen," Lee cautioned her in a gentle tone. "Her death resulted from eclampsia in labor. It's very tragic. She had convulsions, then fell into a coma. Yvette passed away without ever seeing her son. That was a week ago. The baby wasn't released from the hospital until after the funeral.

"It was the grandmother who took him home with her. So far she has refused to let Philippe see his son because she blames him for her daughter's death."

Kellie's groan reverberated throughout the living room. She could hardly comprehend it, or the guilt he must be suffering unnecessarily. *"My poor darling husband,"* her voice shook.

"He's in agony, but he won't talk about it."

"What do you mean?"

"After you left him, he cut himself off from everyone. His family couldn't get through to him. His brother Patrick left Paris to take over for him at the office.

"Raoul is the only person Philippe has let into your apartment. My husband was shocked to discover he hasn't been eating or taking care of himself for the last month. Apparently he's lost at least ten pounds, maybe more.

"But the thing that alarmed Raoul most was to learn from the maid that your husband was getting his climbing gear together. When Raoul asked him what was going on, he said he was planning an ascent of the Matterhorn this weekend."

"He can't!" Kellie blurted in anguish. "Claudine told me he's still recovering from surgery on his knee."

"She's right. But he's beyond listening to reason. Somehow Raoul managed to get him to agree to wait until the bankers' conference was over so he and Roger and Yves could go with him.

"The guys have a plan to do everything in their power to prevent him from trying anything dangerous. Unfortunately my husband hasn't ever seen Philippe like this before. He isn't sure they'll be able to stop him."

At this point Kellie's whole body was trembling. "I've got to go to him! It was only because of Yvette's love and need for him that I initiated the divorce. Nothing could keep me away from him now. I love him so desperately you'll never know."

"I think I do. Raoul and I feel you're the only one who can make a difference. That's why I came. To fly you back to Switzerland with me tonight in Raoul's private jet. I rented a car at Sea-Tac airport. We can drive to Seattle whenever you're ready.''

What wonderful people they were.

''Thank you for your generosity, but I couldn't accept your offer,'' she whispered, fighting tears. ''I'll arrange for a commercial flight just as soon as I let my family know.''

Lee got to her feet. ''Kellie? Before you turn me down, there *is* one more thing you should be aware of.''

Sickness welled up in Kellie's throat. ''What is it?''

The princess seemed almost hesitant. ''Philippe has changed.''

''In what way?''

''He *wants* the divorce now.''

She was trying to understand. ''Now? But if Yvette's no longer alive...''

When Lee didn't say anything else, the significance of her words started to sink in.

Kellie felt the room tilt. She clung to the first available chair. Lee was at her side in an instant.

''You look ill. Sit down.''

When Kellie was seated, Lee knelt next to her. She stared into her eyes. ''Tell me what caused you to almost pass out. Surely you must have realized what your continual rejection was doing to him? Sending Philippe those divorce papers absolutely shattered him.''

Lee's gentleness and sincerity slipped past her defenses. Tears gushed down her cheeks.

''I was t-trying to bow out so he could do the right thing for Yvette and his baby. Now to hear that she's gone, a-and he doesn't want me back—you see I've just learned that I'm pregnant with his baby.''

It was Lee's turn to let out a soft gasp before putting her arm around Kellie's shoulders. Several minutes went by while Kellie tried to come to terms with what the princess had told her.

"D-do you know if he's already signed the papers?"

"Not yet. Raoul talked him into waiting until after they'd made their supposed climb, when he had a clearer head."

"Oh, Lee—" She fought to break down sobbing. "What am I going to do?"

There was a long silence. "What do you *want* to do?"

"I want my husband back, but I don't want to use the news that we're having a baby to be the reason he doesn't go through with the divorce."

"I wouldn't want that, either."

"What if he refuses to see me?"

"There has to be a way. But as I told you before, he's not the same man."

Kellie got up from the chair. "Then I'm going to have to fight for his love because I can't lose him!"

Lee rose to her feet. "I'm glad to hear you say that because it *is* going to be a fight." She opened her handbag and pulled out what looked like a newspaper clipping. "Read this, then you'll understand part of your husband's turmoil."

With trembling fingers Kellie unfolded it to discover the front page of a major French-Swiss newspaper. The date September 30 stood out as if it had been stamped in red ink.

On the bottom half was a picture of Philippe's car jammed against a van. There was a smaller picture of him in a business suit. Kellie's shock turned to horror as she started to read the accompanying story.

Last night an accident sent well-known wealthy French auto-magnate Philippe Didier and an unidentified pregnant woman to Vaudois Hospital in Neuchâtel. Hospital authorities would not give out details, but it's rumored that Kellie Didier, the new American bride of Monsieur Didier has fled the country. Speculation of an affair between M. Didie—

A moan escaped Kellie's throat. She couldn't read anymore and handed it back to Lee. "I—I had no idea—"

"Forgive me, Kellie, but Raoul made me promise I would show this to you if you decided to fly back with me. First, he wanted you to understand what Philippe has been forced to deal with on top of everything else.

"Secondly he says you need to be prepared for an invasion of the press. If you arrive with me, you can clear customs on board the jet. Raoul will have a limousine waiting to drive us to the château. He'll make certain there aren't any journalists around. That way you can slip back in the country without being bombarded with questions and camera flashes."

She took a shaky breath. "How can I ever repay you and the prince for all this?"

Lee's gaze searched hers. "If you and Philippe can works things out and be happy again, it's the only payment we want. We've been looking forward to meeting the woman who brought Philippe to his knees."

"I'm afraid it's always been the other way around," Kellie whispered in pain. "After what you've told me, getting on my knees isn't going to be nearly enough."

"Love will find a way."

"I pray that's true because I love him more than life itself!"

They regarded each other for a long moment before

Lee said, "You have to admit it's an amazing coincidence that our husbands married American women. To find out you and I are the same nationality has been so exciting for me."

"Me, too. The truth is, Philippe and I could hardly wait for you to return from your honeymoon. We had this whole evening planned to welcome you back and really get acquainted."

"So did we! You should hear Raoul talk about all the things the four of us are going to do together in the future."

"If there is one," Kellie's voice broke.

Lee's expression sobered. "When we found out you were divorcing him, you have no idea what a crushing blow it was to us. My husband has taken it very hard. He'll do anything to facilitate a reunion."

"Your presence here is testimony of that fact. Philippe's blessed to have such friends. He told me about the time Raoul saved him on the mountain. Now you're here to rescue him again."

"It's no more than Philippe did for Raoul."

"What do you mean?"

"If it weren't for your husband, Raoul and I would never have met. I'll tell you about it on the plane."

"I want to hear everything. Please excuse me while I talk to my family and pack. I'll try not to take long."

"Don't worry. In the meantime, I'll call my husband and let him know what's happening."

"Come in my grandfather's den where there's a phone and you can have your privacy."

Thirteen hours later their private jet landed in Geneva where the official came on board to stamp their passports. When he left, Lee and Kellie went out to the black limousine bearing the D'Arillac royal crest. It sat parked a few feet beyond the stairs. The tinted glass prevented anyone from seeing inside.

One of the stewards stowed their bags in the trunk while Kellie followed Lee into the back of the limo. The door closed and they were off to Neuchâtel.

"*Petite—*" she heard the prince cry an endearment before pulling his wife into his arms.

Kellie took the seat opposite them and tried to look anywhere else while he kissed her. Talk about two people in love! They reminded her so much of the way it had once been between her and Philippe, she was wounded all over again.

"Raoul, darling?" she heard Lee finally say in a husky voice. "Meet Kellie Didier."

"How do you do, your highness."

His brilliant blue gaze flicked to Kellie. "Please—call me Raoul," he said in English with hardly a trace of accent. With one arm still hugging his wife tightly, he clasped Kellie's hand for a moment before letting go. "Thank God you came. Philippe is badly in need of his wife."

Kellie struggled not to fall apart. "I need him even more. Thanks to you and the princess, I know what's happened. You have no idea how grateful I am for all you've done to make this easier for me. As I told your wife, someday I'll find a way to repay you."

A grave expression spread over his attractive features. "The only thing of importance is that you're here now. You *do* understand his fragile emotional state?" he asked with an underlying trace of demand.

She couldn't blame him for being protective of his best friend. In fact she loved him for it.

"Darling," Lee cautioned softly. "Kellie's in a pretty fragile state herself."

"What do you mean?"

"You didn't tell him?" Kellie asked her.

Lee shook her head. "I didn't think it was my place."

Raoul stared at Kellie. "Tell me what?"

"I found out I'm going to have a baby."

He shook his handsome dark-blond head. "Unbelievable."

Her news had shocked him. But not as much as it had shocked Kellie who still couldn't comprehend the fact that she was going to be a mother.

"I should be congratulating you," he added. "Instead all I can think of is that when Philippe hears the news, he'll believe it's the only reason you came to Switzerland."

"I'm way ahead of you," Kellie's voice shook. "That's why he mustn't be told about it until—until—"

"How can we help?" he broke in.

"You've already done so much, I'm ashamed."

"Kellie— I know in my gut you and Philippe would do the same thing for us if our positions were reversed."

"Of course we would," she avowed. "Philippe looks on you as a brother."

"The feeling's mutual so there'll be no more talk on that score." He sat back in the seat while he clung to his wife. "Do you have a plan of what you want to do first? It goes without saying that our home is at your disposal."

"Thank you." She smoothed the hair out of her eyes. "During the flight I thought of several ways to approach him, but in the end I was afraid they'd all fail. Then

Lee told me about Philippe's plan to help you when you found out your marriage date to Princess Sophie had been brought forward. That's when an idea came to me.''

''What a black day that was,'' he confessed.

''As I understand it, Philippe talked you into luring the princess to your chalet in Zermatt with the hope she'd call off your wedding when she found out the two of you had nothing in common.''

Raoul nodded before smiling at his wife. ''Then you showed up in her place.'' He kissed her again.

Kellie cleared her throat. ''I—I was thinking we might try his strategy in reverse?''

The prince was quick on the uptake. He turned his head and looked at Kellie with a shrewd regard. ''So Philippe shows up at the chalet before the climb and finds you in residence.''

''Yes. For one thing, it might be better for us to meet on neutral ground where we're away from his work or any associations to do with us. The apartment has too many memories that could tear both of us apart.

''For another, I left my keys on the dresser before I left Neuchâtel. I'd have to ask the concierge to let me in the apartment. He'd probably warn Philippe firs—''

''There's no probably about it. The penthouse has become a fortress,'' Raoul was swift to respond. It gave Kellie a deeper glimpse into Philippe's tortured psyche. She shivered at the uphill battle ahead of her.

''Beyond surprising my husband at your chalet, I don't have any other ideas yet.''

''As far as I'm concerned, you're as inspired as Philippe was,'' Raoul murmured.

She bit her lip. ''I'm not at all certain it will work, but since he was already planning a climb, he won't be suspecting any subterfuge. If the only thing I accomplish is to prevent him from going up on the mountain in his condition, I'll be thankful.''

''We all will, believe me,'' Raoul said in an emotion-filled voice.

''There's only one problem. Philippe's going to realize you made this possible for me. I couldn't bear it if he turned on you. You're his dearest friend.''

Raoul eyed her with a glint of what looked like admiration. ''Let me worry about that.''

''When is your banking conference over?''

''Today's the final day. My suggestion is that you and Lee get some sleep while I'm in attendance. I should be through around four-thirty. We'll fly to Zermatt in the helicopter and spend the night. I'll give the staff a few days off.

''Tomorrow morning I'll have Philippe flown in. After I bring him to the chalet, I'll conveniently disappear and the rest of us will wait things out at Roger's condo.''

Tomorrow Kellie would see Philippe.

Her heart thudded so hard with excitement and anxiety all rolled into one, she feared something was wrong with it.

Lee moved forward to touch her arm in concern. ''Are you all right?''

She let out a shaky breath. ''There's a strong possibility he won't let me into his life again. I'm petrified our marriage could really be over.''

When neither of them refuted that statement, her fear escalated.

Weary both physically and emotionally, she rested her head against the back of the seat. Her eyelids felt heavy. Before they closed, the last thing she saw was Raoul's grave countenance.

Like a revelation it came to her he knew things about Philippe he hadn't told his wife or Kellie. She didn't know what exactly, but a frisson of terror attacked her body worse than before.

CHAPTER THREE

KELLIE walked Raoul and Lee to the back door of the chalet to see them off.

"I'll be praying for you," Lee whispered, giving Kellie a hug.

"Thank you. I'm going to need it."

Raoul placed his hands on her shoulders. "You have my cell phone number. Call us at anytime."

She nodded.

His eyes looked a darker blue beneath the overcast sky. "Do your magic as only you know how to do."

Kellie let out a half sob. "I'm afraid I've destroyed that for him. But if loving him desperately counts for anything—"

"It counts." He kissed her forehead before throwing an arm around his wife's waist to walk her to the car. It was one of those little electric ones, the only kind allowed to get around Zermatt.

She watched until their car disappeared down the slope. Then she ran through the hallway to the front of the rustic chalet where the picture window gave out on the Swiss resort town famous for its skiing and mountaineering.

Raoul had told her that in good weather she'd be able to view the Matterhorn. Kellie had never been to Zermatt, and had always wanted to see the mountain. But this morning it was shrouded in gray mist.

Another reason why she wouldn't allow Philippe to

attempt a climb, she'd do anything to prevent him from leaving.

She propped herself on the couch near the window trying to imagine what she'd say to him when he arrived. When an hour had passed and there was no sign of the car yet, she began to worry that bad weather might have prevented the helicopter from landing.

However if that were true, Raoul would have phoned to let her know there'd been a delay.

Her gaze wandered to the end of the room where a circular staircase wound its way to the loft. Philippe had spent many nights up there before a climb, or a day of skiing.

She'd been put in the guest bedroom on the main floor. Though she knew it was impossible, there was still this tiny part of her that fantasized about a reconciliation. After a month's deprivation, she was dying with love for him. Whenever she thought about them sleeping together, she could hardly breathe.

Too nervous to sit still, she walked to the bathroom down the hall and ran the brush through her hair one more time. She'd put on tan wool pants and a cream-colored cable-knit sweater he hadn't seen her in before. They were colors he particularly liked on her.

But as she looked at herself in the mirror, she remembered what Lee had said.

Philippe has changed. He wants the divorce now.

A sharp pain pierced her heart to realize he wouldn't care what she was wearing because he wasn't going to look at her the same way again.

Almost immobilized by the fears plaguing her, she hurried from the bathroom to the kitchen at the rear of the chalet. From the window over the sink she'd be able to see Philippe arrive.

Earlier she'd prepared fruit and ham and cheese croissants for him. The coffee was hot. She knew he'd lost weight during the last month, but was determined to get him to eat.

She wanted to do everything for him.

She wanted to be all things to him.

She wanted to be his wife again.

It had been so long…

Just when she decided something had gone wrong and Philippe wouldn't be coming, she heard the sound of a car.

With her heart pounding out of control, she moved to the side of the sink where she could still see out the window without being observed in return.

Pretty soon she saw it pull around the slope and stop about thirty feet from the back door. The plan was for Raoul to let Philippe out and tell him to go inside the unlocked door while Raoul did a quick errand he'd remembered at the last minute.

So far it seemed to be working. Raoul kept the car running, but by this time her eyes were riveted on the man climbing out of the passenger seat.

If she hadn't known it was Philippe, she wouldn't have recognized him. His black hair was overly long. In the last month he'd grown a moustache and beard.

He'd always been heartbreakingly handsome to her. He still was, but in an entirely different way. The change in him fascinated and terrified her all at the same time. She felt distanced from him by his outward appearance; it was symbolic of the trauma he'd experienced in the last month.

Six feet two inches of powerful muscle beneath his climbing clothes, the noticeable weight loss gave him a lean, hungry look. Kellie was so mesmerized by the transformation, she hardly noticed the cane he used to help keep the weight off his left leg.

His limp appeared almost nonexistent. Once again she found herself thanking providence that he hadn't sustained worse injuries in the accident.

Raoul waved to him, then took off. Philippe gave a slight nod before walking the rest of the way to the chalet.

As she heard the back door open and close, perspiration broke out on her brow. Her body went hot, then cold.

She detected the slight tap of his cane as he walked down the hall past the kitchen. Then suddenly, everything went quiet.

He'd seen her.

On unsteady legs, Kellie crossed the distance to the doorway, coming face to face with a man who bore a superficial resemblance to the husband she adored. But this close to him, those dark slits glittering with accusation couldn't be his eyes.

Beneath his facial hair, the features she loved so well looked chiseled in stone. Combined with his forbidding stance, she sought the doorjamb for support.

"You should have come to the apartment instead of using Raoul to get to me," he said in a wintry voice she didn't recognize. "I would have signed those divorce papers before showing you the door."

Dear God.

"As it is, you'll have to go back where you came from and wait five more days for your long-sought freedom."

"Philippe—"

"I suppose I shouldn't be surprised you would stoop so low as to presume on my relationship with the prince in order to achieve your own ends. To think there was a time when I thought I knew you…"

His hostility went beyond anything she could have imagined. How in heaven would she be able to break through the formidable barrier he'd erected against her?

"Please, sweetheart—we have to talk."

"Don't." His quiet rage was more terrifying than if he'd shoved her body against the wall. "I'll give you ten minutes to leave the chalet. That's nine minutes and thirty seconds more than you gave me in the E.R."

Every word cut her like a knife before he jerked away from her. What happened next was like something out of a ghastly nightmare.

Tossing his cane aside, he started up the back staircase two steps at a time, the way he would have done before the accident.

"No!" she screamed, chasing after him, but he was too fast for her. As he reached the top, she saw him trip. He fell against the floor groaning in agony.

"Darling!" She flew the rest of the distance and knelt at his side where he was half-sitting half-lying there holding his bad leg. As much as she wanted to touch him, comfort him, she didn't dare. "Don't move. I'll call for help."

Already she could see perspiration beading his hairline. Pain had drawn the color from his complexion.

He flashed her a withering glance. "I told you to get out!"

No way.

"This isn't your house, Philippe. I have as much right to be here as you do. Right now you need medical help."

Without waiting to take anymore of his cruel rejection, she hurried back down the stairs to her room.

Raoul had left his cell phone number on the end table next to the guest phone.

She grabbed the receiver and punched the digits. To her relief he responded on the second ring.

"Raoul— I'm so glad you answered!"

"Kellie? I haven't even reached Roger's yet. What's wrong? You sound out of breath." There was alarm in his voice.

"Philippe has hurt his leg." In the next few seconds she related what had happened.

"Your magic worked even faster than I thought it would. There'll be no climbing for him in the foreseeable future, thank God. I'll bring the doctor."

"All right. Please hurry. He's in pain."

"That's good. It means he's feeling again," Raoul murmured before clicking off.

Pondering that comment, Kellie hurried into the kitchen to fashion a makeshift ice bag.

As she rummaged around in the drawers for some plastic bags, it dawned on her once again how fortunate they were to be Raoul's guests. In fact she agreed with their host that this latest accident was a blessing in disguise.

But when a stream of bitter French invective penetrated to the hall, it didn't prevent her from shivering all the way to the loft to rejoin her husband.

By the time she reached him, he'd dragged himself to the nearest bed and had collapsed on top of it. If she hadn't had the advantage for the moment, his withering regard would have paralyzed her.

She walked past him to pull a pillow from each of the other three beds. "Here. Let's get these under your knee."

The fact that he let her arrange the pillows to elevate

his trousered leg indicated his degree of agony. She followed that action with the ice bag which she placed over his knee.

Without asking his permission, she unlaced his boot and carefully pulled it off. She repeated the process with his other boot. To be able to take care of him again in any capacity filled her with inexpressible joy.

It was an automatic gesture to put the back of her hand to his forehead. "You're hot, darling. Let me help you off with this sweater."

Because he hadn't tried to interfere with her ministrations, she didn't think he would fight her for taking this liberty, too.

That's where she was wrong.

As she started to ease it from his hips, his right hand seized her wrist in a viselike grip, hurting her. She'd forgotten he had muscles of whipcord strength.

"You've done enough. Do you understand?"

He shook off her hand as if it were something hateful. She chose to pretend she hadn't noticed his rough treatment of her.

"I'll find you some painkillers."

When she eventually emerged from the upstairs bathroom with pills and a glass of water, the doctor had already entered the loft. There was no sign of Raoul.

The elderly man was bent over Philippe asking him questions while he rolled up his pant leg to survey the damage. When she approached the bed, he lifted his gray head to nod at her.

"*Frau Didier?* I'm Dr. Glatz," he said in heavily accented English.

"How do you do, Doctor. Thank you for coming so quickly. My husband's in pain."

"When I heard he was still recovering from knee

surgery, I realized he needed to be seen immediately. However my examination shows that no new injury has occurred from his fall.

"What he has done is jar those tender nerve endings that have been healing. A few days of bed rest and he'll be fine. As long as you help him walk to the bathroom, there should be no problem."

"I'm so thankful!" she cried in relief.

"You've done an excellent job of first-aid. Are you a nurse?"

She shook her head. "No. I just did what I thought would feel good to me."

"Your instincts do you proud." He peered at the pills in her hand. "Go ahead and give him three of those every four hours. I'll leave something stronger in case the pain intensifies.

"The best thing is the ice pack. Twenty minutes on, twenty minutes off. If you keep up the rotation throughout the night, he'll improve that much faster."

Thank you, Doctor. You've just granted me a stay of execution for another twelve hours. If I could kiss you, I would.

"*Herr Didier?*" He patted her husband's broad shoulder. Philippe lay there staring at her with an almost menacing look coming from his shuttered eyes. "I leave you in the capable hands of your beautiful wife."

In an aside he said, "My bag's in the kitchen. I'll put the medicine on the counter with my card and see myself out. Call me if there's any further problem."

"I will. Thank you again! Goodbye."

"Goodbye."

No doubt Raoul was outside waiting to drive him back to his office or clinic, and Philippe knew it.

Kellie walked over to his side. ''You heard the doctor. Take these now.''

She extended her hand to put them in his mouth. The contact of his lips against her fingers sent an intense wave of longing through her body. She steeled herself not to show how his touch had affected her.

When she handed him the glass of water, his hand trembled as he drained it. Maybe he'd been affected by their brief physical encounter. Then again his reaction could be attributed to natural weakness now that he's survived the initial pain.

He gave her the empty glass without thanking her. Not that she expected it. But in the past her husband had always been the ultimate gentleman. Because of her decision to divorce him, that man no longer existed. Another pain squeezed her heart.

If she could find a way to get him to listen to her. Really listen while she tried to make him understand that it was because she loved him so much, she'd been willing to give him up.

''Philippe?'' she ventured in a quiet voice.

''Have the decency to leave me alone.''

His cold rebuke was devastating to her. She averted her eyes from the sensuous male mouth she yearned to feel on her own. Somehow she had to learn how to stop the bleeding every time one of his daggers found its mark.

''I'll take this ice bag downstairs and bring another one back in twenty minutes.''

When she reached the hall below, she picked up his cane and hung it on one of the pegs next to the back door. In the kitchen she made up half a dozen ice bags which she left in the freezer so they'd be ready.

Following that, she prepared a tray of food. In case

the pills upset his stomach, she added an icy cold bottle of soda to settle it.

Thankful Philippe had to follow the doctor's regimen if he wanted a quick recovery, she went back upstairs. This time she found him asleep.

He'd removed his sweater. It lay on the floor in a heap. The well-defined chest beneath his black T-shirt was still visible, but she was troubled by his weight loss.

She set the tray on the nightstand and placed a new ice bag over his knee. The cold caused him to stir, then his eyes opened. For a fraction of a second she thought she saw a flicker of something that reminded her of the old Philippe. But it was probably her imagination.

"It's lunchtime. I've brought you some food in case you're hungry."

"I'm not."

Alarmed, she asked, "Are you nauseous?"

His lips twisted unpleasantly. "I wasn't..." He left her to surmise what he'd really meant.

It hurt. It hurt so much she could hardly function. But she'd be damned if she'd let it show.

"In that case the soda should do you some good. I've already removed the lid." She put it on the edge of the table. "Here it is within reach of your hand."

Gathering up his sweater, she folded it and put it in one of the empty dresser drawers opposite his bed. "I'll come back later." She left the room leading with her chin.

The next time she looked in on him to remove the bag, she noticed with satisfaction he'd drunk most of the soda and had eaten part of a croissant.

When she went downstairs again she discovered Raoul waiting for her with a smile on his face. He'd brought in Philippe's backpack, which contained items he'd need.

"The guys are staying at Roger's until tomorrow," he whispered. "Lee and I will sleep at the Alex hotel. Call me if you need help."

"I probably will because I don't know what I'm doing from one moment to the next."

He eyed the partially eaten croissant on the tray she'd brought down with her. "From my vantage point it looks like huge strides have already been made."

"You wouldn't say that if you could hear the way he speaks to me. *Or doesn't,*" she lamented in a tremulous whisper.

"I have every confidence in you, Kellie."

"I wish *I* did. He believes I deliberately used you to get to him. It's not far from the truth," she half sobbed. "H-he despises me for it."

"One day I'll let him know I sent Lee on a mission. For the time being it's better to let him think what he wants. He needs that anger to cling to."

"What do you mean?"

"Your husband's a proud man who's been left alone long enough to convince himself you never loved him."

Though it pained her to admit her actions had brought about this horrendous situation, she realized he'd spoken the truth. "Somehow I'll have to prove my love all over again."

"The guys have their bets placed on you. As far as Lee and I are concerned, I think you know how we feel."

She gave him a hug with her free arm. "I do. Thank you for everything."

"Good luck."

Kellie would need good luck.

Throughout the rest of the day she alternated between tending to Philippe's ice bags and preparing some homemade food.

At cooking school she'd developed a special recipe for vichyssoise. She served it warm and followed it with lime escalope de veau and shelled peas seasoned with thyme and steamed slowly over a layer of lettuce to enhance their flavor. The meal had won her first prize during the school's final week of cooking competitions.

This would be the first time she'd prepared it for Philippe. During their first month of marriage, their *only* month she moaned inwardly, any free time she'd had left over from her French studies was devoted to her gorgeous husband.

Prior to the their marriage, he'd retained a cook who came in several times a week to order food and prepare meals. All that changed when he brought Kellie back to Neuchâtel as his wife. She insisted on doing the shopping and the cooking herself.

More often than not however, she would pick him up after work and they'd drive into the countryside dotted with chalets in flowering meadows and the occasional castle hugging a steep, verdant hillside.

They'd share a romantic meal at some charming local restaurant famous for its raclette or fondue dishes. After a short walk, they'd return home for a night of rapture in each other's arms.

Not tonight.

Maybe not ever again.

But that thought was so insupportable, she refused to entertain it any longer.

To think negatively was an exercise in wasted energy. She'd come to Switzerland to save her marriage. The first thing to do was forget herself and concentrate on *his* needs.

It would mean fighting fire with fire, but there was no other option.

With her mind made up, a plan began to form. Full of determination, she returned the tray to the kitchen. After plucking the cane from the peg, she carried it upstairs along with Philippe's backpack and the plastic bottle of pills the doctor had left.

Philippe's eyes were closed, but he could be pretending in order to blot her from his consciousness. After lying on that bed all day, he was probably wide awake and in the kind of pain he would never admit to her.

She walked over to the next bed and emptied his backpack. Once she'd found the kit containing his toiletries, she took it to the bathroom and laid everything out on the counter for him.

A few minutes later she approached him and removed the ice bag. "Philippe? It's time to help you to the bathroom."

His dark-lashed eyelids flew open so fast, she realized she'd been right in her assessment about his determination to ignore her existence.

"I'll help ease your leg to the floor. Here's your cane. Use it to inch your way to the edge of the bed. When you're ready to stand, put your other arm around my shoulder."

Pleased that he didn't protest, she waited until he was ready, then bent her knees so he could slide his arm around her.

If she'd needed further evidence of his revulsion of her, his taut masculine physique was the proof. His body might as well have been an unyielding block of cement.

The second he reached the bathroom, he removed his arm from her shoulder and disappeared inside, slamming the door in her face. Not to be thwarted, she straightened his bedding and found another pillow to support his head.

When he finally emerged with his cane, the venomous look in his eyes challenged her to take one step toward him. Deciding that he seemed to be managing all right, she stayed where she was. Not until he sat down did she help lift his leg onto the pillows which she arranged once he'd fallen back against the mattress.

She rested his cane against the side of the nightstand so he could reach it if he needed to. Then she pulled one of the chairs near his bed and sat down.

"I know you hate my being here, and wish we were already divorced," she began before he could order her out of the loft, "but it's fortunate you haven't signed those papers yet."

His emotional withdrawal seemed even more pronounced.

"I say that because you need a wife to help you gain custody of your son. Yvette's mother may love her grandson, but she's not the parent and has no right to keep him from you. We're still married, Philippe," she declared in a firm voice.

"Together we can convince a judge we have a stable home complete with a mother and father who want nothing more than to raise our child."

"Mon Dieu!" he lashed out in rage. "You think for one second you could convince a judge of anything after the headlines let the whole world know you disappeared off the face of the earth at the first sign of trouble in the Didier marriage?"

Don't let his fury get to you now, Kellie.

Raoul had known what he was doing when he'd wanted her to see that newspaper article first.

"Yes. Judges rule for the welfare of the child, nothing else. When he hears that I was willing to give you your freedom so you could marry Yvette to give your son your name and provide a home, it will weigh the case in our favor.

"Especially when I tell him that there was no divorce because the birth mother passed away and now I've come back to help raise the baby as if it had been born from my own body."

He made a noise that sounded of bitterness and so many other violent emotions she couldn't decipher them all.

"All he'd need to see is the letter I left in the study for you as proof of my intentions."

Philippe jackknifed into a sitting position on the bed, mindless of the pain it must be causing him. "You think that letter still exists?" The words came out sounding like a hiss.

She wasn't going to let him get to her. "It doesn't matter. I told Claudine everything I wrote to you."

"There's been no DNA test done yet. It may turn out I'm *not* the father."

"No matter what, Yvette believed it was yours. If you still want the baby, we'll raise it with all the love we have to give."

A grimace transformed his features. "Aside from the fact that her mother would never allow it, are you trying to tell me you'd bring up an infant that wasn't either of ours?" he demanded with such mocking incredulity, she was heartbroken all over again.

"Of course. What if none of this had happened and we'd found out we had to adopt? A baby is a baby,

Philippe. They're so innocent. All they want is love. Did you ever see him?"

There was a long silence. "Once, from the nursery window, but he was too far away for me to form any impression."

"All the same, can you deny your heart didn't melt?"

"It's a moot point if the baby isn't mine."

"Not necessarily. If you'll obey the doctor, the sooner you'll be ready to fly back to Neuchâtel and see what can be done about the situation."

Though Kellie felt it would be better for him to wait a week before he tried to get around again, she knew her husband. He would never be able to stand that much inactivity.

Afraid she'd said too much, she decided to leave before he hurt her with another soul-destroying gibe. She got up from the chair and placed it against the wall.

On the hope that he might phone Raoul to talk things over with him first, she put the cell phone from his backpack on the nightstand next to him.

"I'll be up in a little while with another ice bag."

Afraid her emotions were showing, she hurried down the stairs to finish cooking dinner. But when she entered the kitchen, fatigue seemed to overtake her body.

Since leaving Washington, her headaches had mysteriously stopped. In their place she was aware of an increase in her appetite. Right now she found she was starving to the point that she had the shakes.

Without conscious thought she ate some soup from the serving spoon. It tasted so good she ended up eating two helpings of everything she'd prepared. As she speared the last few peas and put them into her mouth, she remembered the old adage about "eating for two."

Though it had been two weeks since the doctor had

informed her she was going to have a baby, it hadn't seemed real. Not when she'd been expending all her thoughts and energy on her husband who lived across the Atlantic.

Now suddenly she was vitally aware of her condition and would give anything in the world to run upstairs and share the news with him. But she didn't dare do anything to exacerbate an already impossible situation.

Soon she had his plate ready. She prepared sweet hot tea with lemon and put it on the tray with his dinner. Tucking another ice bag under her arm, she carried his meal upstairs.

To her satisfaction he'd managed to prop his back against the headboard and still keep his leg elevated at the same time. He was talking to someone on the phone in a low voice, possibly Marcel. She couldn't make out words. Then again it might be Raoul or his friends, even someone in his family.

She didn't care. His body language let her know he wasn't holding himself as rigidly as before. The pain pills had to be partially responsible for his more relaxed position. But the fact that he was breaking his long silence with the outside world told its own tale.

Taking full advantage of the moment, she put the tray on his lap and laid the ice bag over his knee. Then she hurried downstairs so he couldn't accuse her of eavesdropping.

If he didn't want his dinner, he'd have to try to put the tray on the nightstand. She was counting on it being too difficult for him to attempt. In twenty minutes she'd go back to remove the ice bag and discover if her efforts had been wasted.

Kellie had seen the anguish in his eyes when she'd brought up the subject of Yvette's mother keeping his son from him. More than ever she was determined to help him. Getting him to eat was a start in the right direction.

Thirty minutes later she reentered the loft and immediately felt her husband's dark, penetrating gaze. The cell phone lay at his side.

She walked over to the bed. As she removed the ice bag, her eyes couldn't help but wander to the empty dishes on the tray.

"You don't need to look surprised," his voice grated. "I *am* still married to a French chef. There's no point in pretending that it wasn't one of the best meals I've ever eaten."

"Thank you," she whispered, relieved that his appetite seemed to have returned, at least for today. She picked up the tray. "Is there anything else I can do for you?"

"No. You've done quite enough. Don't come up here again."

His cold edict shriveled her heart. Philippe didn't want her anywhere around.

Lee had made Kellie promise to phone if she needed to talk. Now was one of those times, but when she tried the number it was busy.

An hour later, after cleaning up the kitchen, she went to the bedroom and pressed the buttons again.

"Put the receiver back on the hook."

Kellie spun around in shock. Philippe had entered the room in his bare feet. He leaned on his cane.

"What possessed you to attempt those stairs?" she cried out. "Don't you want your knee to get better?"

"Thanks to your expert nursing care, it feels fine. Hang up the phone, Kellie."

Her fingers obeyed his command.

"Once before you did a disappearing act on me."

Heat swept into her face, scorching her cheeks.

"Guilty as sin, aren't you. It seems you have no shame."

Though his bitter mockery stung her to the quick, all she could think about was his leg and how much it must be hurting.

"Philippe—you need to lie down."

His eyes narrowed. "If you're suggesting I go to bed in here, I have no complaint. It's either this room or the master bedroom."

Ignoring his taunt she said, "Please rest your leg and let me make you comfortable."

"Is that an invitation?" He sneered at her.

"Don't be ridiculous. I want to wait on you."

"Today you gave me help when I needed it most. Tonight's a different story."

Kellie willed herself not to rise to the bait. "If you're feeling that much better, I'll phone for a taxi and leave."

"Fine. I'll call Honore and cancel our appointment with him for tomorrow."

He'd already talked to him?

Honore Dufort, the Didier family solicitor had been like another member of their household. Kellie had grown very fond of him during her month's stay in Paris. After her marriage to Philippe, they'd entertained him at the apartment when he'd come on business.

"But you don't want me here," her voice shook.

"Let's just say I no longer have the desire to sleep with my wife."

Kellie knew that, but to hear it put so bluntly shot excruciating pain through her body.

"Tell me now if you're planning another vanishing act so I can cancel it."

"But the doctor said you shouldn't go anywhere for a couple of days."

His jaw hardened. "Every day I don't take action puts me at a further distance from my child, provided of course that it's mine. The taxi will be here for us at eighty-thirty in the morning to drive us to the helicopter pad. If you're not here when I get up, I'll know you left by some other means."

Philippe wanted Yvette's son. Though he despised Kellie, he wanted the baby enough to use her.

Kellie loved her husband enough to be used.

"I'm so thankful Honore believes you have a chance to win custody of the baby," she said before turning toward the bathroom.

"Kellie?"

She paused midstride. "Yes?"

"If this is some elaborate ploy to try to fix what's wrong between us, then you're wasting your time. Should it turn out this baby is mine and I get custody, you can plan on a divorce as soon as I've found the right live-in nanny.

"In case it isn't mine, I'll sign those divorce papers and put you on a plane back to Washington so fast, you won't have time to blink."

Though he'd meant every word just now, he'd listened to her proposition and wasn't throwing her out of Raoul's chalet tonight. It was something to be thankful for.

From here on she would bide her time until she could find a crack in that frozen wall of ice surrounding his heart. No matter how impossible it looked, she would never stop trying to win back his love.

"Please know that I'll do everything in my power to help you gain custody of your son before you divorce me.

"If, as you said, it's proven he's not your child and you choose not to pursue things further, you have my promise I'll leave you alone."

But I won't promise to leave Switzerland. I can't. Not when I'm carrying your child.

CHAPTER FOUR

THE limousine driver who had picked up Kellie and Philippe at the prince's private heliport in Neuchâtel put their baggage in the apartment lift before he disappeared from the lobby.

Philippe was so fiercely independent, he leaned on his cane and refused any help from her. Nursing him throughout the night with ice bags was one thing. But they were no longer at the chalet.

As they rode to the penthouse, she realized it was better that they didn't touch. Otherwise he'd feel her pulse racing out of control because she was coming back to a place where she'd known ecstasy with her husband.

The second he let them in the door, her eyes darted everywhere while she drank in the familiar ambiance with its attendant memories of living and loving.

As she walked through the rooms, all signs of the intimate dinner for two had been cleared away. Had he instructed the maids to throw everything in the trash? The cuff links and the accompanying note where she'd poured out her love?

Before he could banish her from their bedroom, she headed for the guest room with her overnight bag. He'd made it clear she was here for one reason only. The last thing she wanted to do was alienate him further by attempting to sleep in the same bedroom with him.

Afraid he would accuse her of hovering, she took a shower and slipped on a skirt and sweater. When she'd emptied her overnight bag and put everything away, she walked through the apartment to the kitchen.

A quick inventory revealed an empty refrigerator. Raoul hadn't exaggerated when he'd said Philippe had stopped eating. How could he when there was no food in the place!

Her first order of business was to make a hot pot of tea for husband, then go to the market. Glad for something constructive to do, she opened a tin of biscuits to serve with it, then fashioned another ice bag. When everything was ready, she went in search of him.

"Oh— I'm sorry—"

She'd almost collided with his tall, rock solid physique in the hallway where he'd just come out of their bedroom using his cane. He'd showered and changed into trousers and a pullover in a dark red color she particularly loved against his olive complexion.

"Shouldn't you be resting your leg?"

He stared at the tray, then at her. His lids veiled his eyes so she couldn't tell what he was thinking.

"I'd prefer talking to Patrick in the living room," he muttered before walking around her.

Surprised that his brother was coming here, she followed him to the living room sofa and set the tray down on the coffee table in front of him.

"How soon will he be arriving?" she asked as she propped a cushion under his left leg.

"Any minute now."

"Then I'll hurry with the grocery shopping and make lunch for both of you."

"Don't bother. I'm still full from the breakfast you fixed at the chalet, and Patrick is only making a quick stop on his way to the airport."

"Where's he going?"

''Back to Paris.''

''Is there an emergency of some kind at home?'' she asked in alarm.

His malignant stare crushed her. ''He covered for me while I was incapacitated. Now that I'm able to get back to work, I no longer need his help.''

''I see,'' her voice trailed.

Though she was thrilled by the news, she had ambivalent feelings about his returning to his job while his leg was still bad. But she held back from speaking her mind. The situation was so precarious, it was like walking through a minefield. One false step and all her dreams could explode in her face.

''Let me get another cup from the kitchen so he can at least enjoy some tea with you while I'm out shopping.''

When she returned to the living room, she found him on the phone. He broke off talking to flash her an annoyed glance.

''I'm sorry to disturb. Do you know where my keys are?''

''I imagine where you left them.''

There had been a new change in his behavior since they'd arrived at the apartment. His anger was already a given, but he seemed to have grown bored of her presence. Though she'd tried to immure herself from the pain he inflicted, his uncharacteristic rudeness found her weak spot every time.

She had no choice but to leave him to his own devices while she went to the master bedroom in search of her keys.

They were still on the top of the dresser. As she recalled the hellish events of the night he'd had the accident, her hand squeezed them so tightly, the little silver pickax charm on the key ring drew blood. She hurried into the bathroom to wash everything off and apply a small plaster.

When she'd left the Didier home to return to Washington with Claudine, Philippe had bought it for her so she wouldn't forget him. To her joy he'd shown up at her home a week later. Within a month's time they were married.

While she stood there, memories of the intimacy they'd shared swamped her. But sharp, searing pain followed, causing her to put a hand over her heart as if to numb it.

The irate male in the other room with the dark beard and moustache was a stranger to her. Where once her husband couldn't stand for her to be out of his arms, this man could barely tolerate her existence.

In an abrupt move, she turned away from the sink. If she hoped to make any headway with him, she had to move forward with her plan and stop reliving the past.

Full of determination, she walked over to the bedside table and pulled the telephone directory from the drawer. She opened it to the *B*'s. It didn't take her long to find the only entry for Boiteux. There was an initial *A* next to it. *Analise?* Number ten, rue de Guisan.

Kellie turned to the front of the directory and studied the city map. It didn't take much time for her to locate the rue de Guisan on the northern outskirts of Neuchâtel. She could find it easily enough in her car.

On the way out of the apartment with her shopping bags, she noted that Philippe was drinking his tea while he talked on the phone. As long as he ate what she fixed him, he'd start to gain the weight he'd lost. She ought to be thankful he'd tolerate that much of her help.

She *was* thankful. But now that she was back in their

home, the task that lay ahead of her seemed more insurmountable and treacherous than climbing Mount Everest, the frozen, forbidding natural wonder Philippe had conquered with his friends.

If he noticed her slip out of the apartment on her way to the underground car park, she couldn't tell. Much as she would have liked to visit with Patrick, she knew better than to stay behind and incur her husband's wrath.

Her car had been sitting there for over a month. To her relief the engine turned over without problem. Kellie drove out to the main street and headed for a certain area in the center of town she loved to frequent.

It smelled of freshly baked bread, roasted coffee and cocoa beans. No supermarkets here. Just a series of wonderful shops where she'd become acquainted with the proprietors who sold the freshest dairy products, meat and produce to be found.

Knowing her husband's penchant for a special hazelnut chocolate, she purchased several bars. With her bags filled to the brim, she put them in her car and headed to the north end of town.

After a few wrong turns she finally found the street and ultimately the apartment in question. It was in a newer section where the rent wouldn't be as high.

Once she'd found a space along the main road to park, she locked the car and hurried inside the main entrance of the three-story building with a small bouquet of flowers. She scanned the list of names next to the buzzers of the various tenants, then picked up the wall phone receiver.

Her finger shook as she pressed number four.

It took close to a minute before a woman answered. *"Oui?"*

"Madame Boiteux?"

"Yes. Who is it?" she demanded tersely.

"It's Madame Didier, Philippe's wife."

An ominous silence followed. Kellie feared the older woman would hang up on her.

"We have to meet," she rushed on in French. "You've lost your daughter. I've lost my husband."

"What do you mean?"

Tears filled Kellie's eyes unbidden. "Please let me come in and I'll explain. I know you're in pain, but so am I. If we could talk, we might be able to help each other. I'm not here to cause trouble."

It seemed like an eternity before she heard, "You may come in for a minute. When you hear the bell, enter through the door on the left. My apartment is at the end of the hall."

"Bless you, *madame*."

She hung up the receiver and hurried over to the glass door in question. As soon as she'd gained entrance, she fairly raced down the corridor.

Yvette's mother had opened her door and stood waiting for Kellie. The sturdy Swiss woman with graying hair was probably in her sixties, but her grief-stricken face made her appear older.

Evidently the baby was asleep because she put a finger to her lips as she motioned for Kellie to enter the small living room and sit down. The modestly furnished apartment looked immaculate. Except for an infant carryall in the tiny entrance hall, there were no other signs of the baby.

Kellie studied several photographs of Yvette placed on the end table. Some of them showed her skiing. She'd been an attractive woman with short, dark brown hair, very chic and somewhat older in appearance than Kellie had imagined.

"Thank you for seeing me, *madame.*" She cleared her throat. "First of all, let me tell you how sorry I am about your daughter. I can't imagine anything worse than losing a child. Please accept these flowers as a token of my sympathy."

The older woman's features didn't change, but her gray eyes dimmed. After a slight hesitation, she took the bouquet from Kellie with a muttered thank-you.

"In case you were wondering, my husband has no idea I'm here. I don't even want to think how he'll feel when he finds out, but I had to come. If you'll bear with me, I'd like to start at the beginning. Then maybe you'll understand why I'm here."

The woman's silence seemed to indicate Kellie could continue. Without preamble she told Yvette's mother about the horror of the night when she found out Philippe and Yvette had been in the accident.

"Before we were married, I knew there'd been a few special women in his life. I didn't know their names, but in the E.R. he told me about Yvette. He could have lied to me about her, but he didn't because he's an honorable man.

"I'm sure your daughter was an honorable woman, too," Kellie rushed to assure her. "They got caught in a situation that resulted in a child. I don't blame her for turning to him. She was sick and afraid, and she loved him."

The older woman clasped her hands together. "My daughter met him on a ski trip to Chamonix. He was all she talked about after her return."

"I know. I heard the love in her voice while she begged the doctor to bring Philippe to her. It tore me apart because she was pleading for her baby as well as herself.''

Madame Boiteux averted her eyes.

''The trouble was, I loved him, too, and was faced with the greatest dilemma of my life deciding what I should do. You see, my father abandoned my mother and me before I was born. It was like reliving history. That's when the answer came to me.

''While Philippe was in X ray, I went back to our apartment and wrote him a letter. In it I told him his place was with Yvette because he'd known her first. For that reason I was filing for divorce so he could marry her and they could be a family. Then I left for Washington.''

Her confession caused the other woman's head to rear back. ''You did that for my daughter?''

''For the three of them. If a friend hadn't informed me of Yvette's passing, I would never have come back to Neuchâtel. Do you want to hear something ironic? Now that I've returned, my husband doesn't want me. He doesn't believe I ever loved him.'' Her voice shook. ''But he does want his son, if it *is* his son.

''There's no if, *madame.*''

''I believe you,'' Kellie asserted, ''but you can understand why there might be a question in his mind. Yvette should have come to Philippe with the news the moment she suspected she was pregnant. Instead she waited until we'd been married for a month before she approached him. H-he's going to ask for a DNA test to be done.''

The other woman cringed.

''If you knew Philippe, you'd realize he's in terrible emotional turmoil because he had no idea of Yvette's condition. Whether you realize it or not, he's taken her death very hard. If the test is a match, then he's prepared to do everything for his son.

"I'm here today because I'm prepared to do anything to win back my husband's love. If you could find it in your heart to let us spend some time with the baby, it will help Philippe to heal, and it might even soften his anger toward me."

Looking distraught, Yvette's mother got up from the couch.

"I want to be Philippe's wife again. There's nothing I'd love more than to help him raise the baby. That little boy is innocent and deserves the love of two parents and his grandmother.

"Philippe has the means to support the child, but much more important than money, he loves children and will make the best father in the world.

"At one time he cared something for Yvette or he would never have become intimate with her. She wanted him to help raise their child. That's why she finally turned to him. He's prepared to do it, but he can't do it alone. He needs me, and he needs you.

"If we all joined forces, Yvette's little boy would be surrounded by love. Would you at least consider bringing the baby to our apartment so we could get acquainted with him?

"Philippe would come here, but two days ago he hurt the knee that was operated on. The doctor has ordered him to rest his leg as much as possible until it's better."

The older woman shook her head. "I can't forgive him."

"You mean because he didn't love Yvette enough to ask her to marry him?"

"Yes!" she cried in pain.

Kellie got to her feet. "Madame? I've found out the

hard way you can't order a person to feel a certain way about anything. I spent years hating my birth father for not marrying my mother and not being a dad to me. In the end it blinded me to reality and cost me my marriage."

"I'm sorry for you." She sounded sincere.

"No more than I am for you. When your grandson gets older, he'll ask about his papa. If he should find out you tried to keep him from the man who begged to be a father to him, then heaven help you.

"Just remember that revenge and anger won't bring Yvette back. But love and forgiveness will help a little boy lead a normal life. Deep down inside, I know that's what Yvette would want for him. I think you know it, too. If you ever got to know Philippe, you'd understand what a wonderful parent he would make."

Afraid she'd break down in front of the older woman she said, "Thank you for allowing me to talk to you. I'll let myself out."

Kellie left the apartment and hurried across the street to her car. The second she got behind the wheel, tears gushed down her cheeks because she saw the same implacable blindness in Analise Boiteux that had crippled her own life.

If Kellie had listened to Claudine, she wouldn't have sent Philippe those awful divorce papers. She would have flown back to Switzerland to be at her husband's side. They would have faced this crisis together. She would have told her husband they were going to have a baby. Now it was all too late...

By the time she reached the apartment, she'd cried herself out and rode the lift dry-eyed with her bags of groceries. After letting herself inside the penthouse, she did a juggling act all the way to the kitchen.

It was after three. Philippe had to be hungry.

She burrowed in the bags and came up with the ingredients for a grilled ham and cheese sandwich. He also loved crenshaw melon. She cut him a large slice, garnished it with lime juice and put everything on a tray.

When she couldn't find him in the living room, she headed for the bedroom. His door was closed. She knocked.

"Philippe?"

"What is it?"

Evidently Patrick's visit hadn't improved his black mood.

"I've made you something to eat. Is it all right if I come in?"

"My brother brought lunch."

That was odd. She hadn't seen any sign of the remains in the living room or the kitchen.

"I have a fresh ice bag for you."

"Put it back in the freezer."

Something was wrong.

Without asking permission, she opened the door and discovered him on top of the bed resting his back against the headboard. Her gaze wandered from the bottle of liquor on the table to the glass in his hand. He must have gotten it from the cabinet in the study.

Philippe rarely drank anything stronger than the occasional beer. More importantly, he never drank alone. It alarmed her to see him this morose.

She walked to the bed, lifted the whiskey bottle onto the tray and placed the whole thing back on the table. Without saying a word, she put the ice bag over his knee and left the room. More than anything in the world she wanted to slam the door, but she wouldn't give him that much satisfaction.

When she reached the kitchen, she had the shakes again and quickly fixed herself a sandwich and a glass of milk. It surprised her to be this hungry again because she'd eaten a huge breakfast at the chalet.

At this rate she was going to put on weight like mad long before the baby was born. Philippe couldn't stand her right now. She dreaded to think how much more she would disgust him when he discovered himself chained to a plump partridge.

Though she was thankful the headaches hadn't come back, she wasn't thrilled about this new manifestation of her pregnancy. As she put all the groceries away, she determined that tomorrow she'd phone Dr. Cutler and find out if there was anything she could do to stem her appetite without hurting the baby.

After she'd retrieved the other tray from the living room, she cleaned things up and started a quiche for dinner. While she was preparing the crust, she heard the phone ring.

It could be anyone. Now that her husband had sent Patrick back to Paris, Marcel might be the one checking in with the boss. Sick at heart for her husband who was suffering, there was no telling what state he'd be in by tomorrow if he stayed in the bedroom and refused to eat.

She finished the quiche and got busy on a special side dish of carrots and parsnips. When everything was ready, she put both casseroles into the oven, hoping the delicious smells would arouse his appetite.

''Kellie?''

Philippe's deep voice was so unexpected, she spun around in surprise. He stood in the doorway leaning on his cane. Maybe he hadn't had that much to drink after all. He seemed steady enough.

"What's wrong?"

His dark eyes swept over her as if he were looking for something he couldn't find.

"That was Analise Boiteux on the phone."

Kellie's heart began to thud mercilessly.

"For some reason I can't fathom, she has decided to let me see the baby. She said it was what Yvette would have wanted her to do."

"Oh, Philippe—"

Analise was a good woman. A *wonderful* woman. Kellie loved her already, and appreciated the fact that Yvette's mother had kept Kellie's visit to her apartment a secret.

"Apparently when she was at the hospital, she heard about the surgery on my knee. She said that if I'd send a taxi for her, she'd bring him here at six this evening."

He looked and sounded stunned. Kellie could imagine what this moment meant to him. At long last he was going to hold his son.

Her first instinct was to offer to pick up Analise and the baby in her car. But she held back out of fear it might be the wrong thing to say.

She couldn't afford to give Philippe any more ammunition to hate her. Not when Analise had risen above her pain to make this momentous gesture. Her phone call was something of a miracle.

"W-would you prefer to be alone for this first meeting?" she stammered. "I can go out for a walk or a drive if yo—"

Lines darkened his face. "So you're running true to form and disappearing at the first sign of trouble? I might have known the valiant speech you made to me about loving an innocent child was nothing more than lip service,'' he lashed out.

''That's not true!'' she cried in anguish, but he'd turned away from her with a swiftness that caught her off guard.

Kellie rushed after him. ''I only said that in case there were things you wanted to discuss with her in private. Philippe—darling—I'll do whatever you ask of me!''

If he heard her, she couldn't tell because he'd slammed the bedroom door in her face.

Needing to do something constructive before she invaded his inner sanctum without permission and made things worse, she hurried into the dining room and set three places for dinner. For a centerpiece she used the other bouquet of flowers she'd bought in town.

Maybe Analise wouldn't want to eat, but Kellie felt it was important to be natural with the older woman so she could see how they lived, what kind of life they had to offer her grandchild.

When everything was ready, she decided to change into a casual café-au-lait colored cotton dress with a rope belt and matching sandals. To her surprise, the zip didn't go up as easily as the last time she'd worn it.

Though no one would guess she was pregnant yet, Kellie was aware of the difference in her measurements. If Philippe ever bothered to really look at her, he would notice the subtle blossoming of her figure.

Before too much more time went by, she needed to tell him about their own baby. *But not tonight.*

After a touch-up of lipstick and a good hair brushing, Kellie made another tour of the apartment to be certain everything looked ready for company.

Like most Swiss women, Analise kept an immaculate apartment. She was probably an excellent cook, too.

Kellie wanted Yvette's mother to see that she also took pride in caring for Philippe and their home.

For one final touch, Kellie went to the linen closet in the hallway and pulled out the handmade quilt her grandmother had given her for a wedding present. It was a solid white whip cream crepe that would fit a double bed.

Because it was a precious heirloom, Kellie hadn't ever used it. But in her mind's eye she could see a baby cuddled up in it. Holding it against her chest, she walked to the living room and folded it over one of the chairs.

It was five after six when she went back to the kitchen to take everything out of the oven. She thought she heard the front door close. That meant Philippe had decided to wait at the elevator anticipating Analise's arrival.

Kellie could only imagine his nervous excitement. Heavens, she was nervous herself! Nature gave you nine months to prepare for a baby growing inside you. But it was quite another matter to be instant parents.

Of course she could be reading way too much into Analise's visit. In fact the more she thought about it, the more she wondered if the mention of the paternity test had made her so angry, she'd decided to come over here without the baby and confront both of them.

A cold chill passed through her body.

It was entirely possible that Kellie's meddling had made things so bad, she'd jeopardized Philippe's chances for any kind of amicable resolution. In that case she wouldn't be surprised if he told her to get out and never come near him again.

It wouldn't matter if she told him they were expecting their own baby. He'd inform her that any further communication would take place through their respective attorneys.

Suddenly her short-lived happiness turned to gut wrenching fear. That enervating weakness she'd suffered in the E.R. had her clinging to the counter. By the time she heard voices coming from the living room, there was a ringing sound in her ears, and her body had gone clammy.

"Kellie?" he called to her.

She couldn't tell by his deep-toned voice if he was angry or not, but it was obvious he expected her to join them.

Shaking like an earth tremor, she left the kitchen and walked through the dining room. At the entrance to the living room she stopped in her tracks.

Two people were standing next to the couch. The woman was familiar to her, but the hard-muscled, dark-haired male holding the baby wasn't the same person who had come to the kitchen a little while ago.

This incredibly handsome man stood tall without his cane. He was clean-shaven and wore a midnight-blue suit toned with a white shirt and striped tie.

The husband she'd married was back.

"Philippe—" she gasped quietly.

CHAPTER FIVE

PHILIPPE must have heard her because he lifted his head.

"Kellie? Come and meet Analise Boiteux," he said in French. "Analise, this is my wife, Kellie."

Again Kellie had the sensation she was floating in some kind of dream unable to control her body parts. She moved awkwardly toward them, still afraid to believe this was really happening.

Analise had come.

She'd brought the baby.

The kind expression in the older woman's eyes made Kellie want to embrace her. Instead she shook hands with her and found herself saying, "I'm enchanted to meet you, *madame.*"

"How do you do?"

Finally Kellie raised her eyes to Philippe's. There was a soft light glowing in those dark depths she hadn't seen since before she'd left Neuchâtel.

"Say hello to Jean-Luc."

Hardly able to breathe, she lowered her eyes to the baby who couldn't weigh more than six or seven pounds and was nestled in the crook of his arm. He had a cap of dark curls and was sleeping soundly.

His adorable little olive-complected face peeked out from the receiving blanket, every feature composed and perfect.

Kellie's heart dissolved. "Oh, Philippe. He's the most precious baby I've ever seen in my life!"

Her tear-filled gaze darted to Analise. "You must be crazy about him."

The other woman's eyes were suspiciously bright. "It's like raising Yvette all over again, only this time I don't have my husband Louis to help me. He would have loved to see his grandchild before he died."

"How long ago did he pass away?"

"Three years."

Without conscious thought Kellie put her hand on Analise's arm. "You've been through so much sadness, but just looking at Jean-Luc must bring you a world of joy. He's so beautiful!"

"Can you hear all the nice things they're saying about you, my son?" Philippe whispered as he stared down at the baby.

My son. That was how Philippe thought of him already.

He'd forgotten all about his knee, but Kellie knew he'd pay the price later and urged Analise to sit so he would.

Once she was seated in the chair, Philippe sank down on the couch. "Do you mind if I take a closer look at him?" he asked Analise.

"I'm surprised you haven't asked before now. Let me get the quilt from the carrya—"

"There's no need, *madame,*" Kellie broke in gently. "I have a quilt right here my grandmother made for us." She reached for it and spread it out on the couch next to Philippe where he placed the baby.

Like unwrapping a fabulous gift, her husband proceeded to undress Jean-Luc with the greatest of care. As he stripped the baby down to his diaper, a smile broke out on his attractive face, the first she'd seen since her arrival in Switzerland.

Kellie got down on her knees in front of the baby to watch. She was fascinated by Yvette's little cherub. Not too far in the future she would be examining her own baby. She couldn't imagine loving it more than she did this one.

The baby's coloring was Philippe's, but the sturdy body and legs led Kellie to believe he wouldn't grow to be as tall or as lean as his father.

Maybe the baby's shape took after Analise's side of the family, or even the men in the Boiteux line. So many ingredients went into the making of a human life.

It was inevitable that Philippe's probing would waken his son. At first his little chin wobbled, then his tiny eyes opened to reveal indistinct grayish brown irises. But there was nothing tentative about the cry he let out, or the way his cute little face screwed up in hunger.

Philippe's low chuckle permeated to Kellie's bones. He leaned over to kiss the baby's tummy. "It's all right. Your papa is here," he murmured to his boy.

With deft hands he changed the baby's diaper, then dressed him and wrapped him back up in his receiving blanket.

"Here." Analise handed him a bottle and a cloth. "You can feed him."

Kellie jumped to her feet and put it over Philippe's broad shoulder. The baby did the rest of the work. He drank his bottle so hard and fast he had all of them laughing, especially when Philippe took the bottle away to burp him and the baby cooperated with a resounding noise.

Much as Kellie longed to hold Jean-Luc, she chose not to interfere. There was no telling how long Analise would agree to stay. Right now it was vital her husband delight in his child for as long as he could.

She turned to Yvette's mother. "Madame Boiteux?"

"Call me Analise."

"Analise?" Kellie said in a quiet tone. "Dinner's ready. If you'd like to follow me into the dining room, we'll eat. Philippe can join us when he's through feeding the baby."

"You're sure it won't be an imposition?"

"Not at all. As soon as he told me you were coming over, I set a place for you."

The two women left Philippe to bond with his son. Kellie could tell he was so absorbed with the baby, he didn't even notice them leave the room.

After urging Analise to sit down at the table, Kellie dashed into the kitchen. Once she'd brought everything in piping hot, she served them.

What she really wanted to do was hug the older woman and pour out her gratitude. But since she didn't know what Analise intended beyond tonight, let alone how she would respond to Kellie's emotional outburst, the only thing left to do was eat. To Kellie's consternation, she was hungry again.

"You have a wonderful cook. I've never tasted such food."

"That's because my wife is a French chef," a familiar male voice responded before Kellie could gather her wits.

Her head whipped around in time to discover that Philippe had entered the dining room. He leaned on his cane with one hand while he balanced the baby on his other arm.

"Is that true?" Analise asked incredulously.

"Yes." Kellie nodded before setting a plate in front of her husband. "My grandparents helped raise me. They own a restaurant and I grew up wanting to run my own one day. A French restaurant, of course, because I think French food is the best.''

When Philippe took his seat at the head of the table he said, ''Every time she prepares a meal, it's better than eating at a five-star restaurant.''

The older woman smiled. ''I've never known a chef. Not every man is so lucky as to have one who also happens to be his wife, *monsieur.*''

His enigmatic gaze passed over Kellie who was warmed by Analise's championing of her.

''I agree, and I hope before this evening is out you'll call me Philippe.''

To Kellie's joy, he began eating with what looked like a hearty appetite. When he'd finished, she served them a raspberry tart and coffee.

''Tell me something, Analise.'' Philippe had just drained his cup. ''Is Jean-Luc always this good? Does he automatically fall asleep after every bottle?''

Her eyes twinkled. ''So far the answer is yes to both questions. Would you like to keep him overnight tonight?''

''Oh could we?'' Kellie blurted before she realized she had no right to say anything at all.

''Of course,'' Analise replied. ''I brought enough formula to last him until tomorrow evening. Everything he'll need is in the diaper bag.''

Philippe put a hand on the older woman's arm. ''You won't be too lonely for him?''

The huskiness in his tone moved Kellie to tears. She got up from the table and started clearing the plates so neither of them would notice how emotional she'd become.

''Oh, I'll miss him,'' Analise came back. ''But you'll never get to know him if you don't take care of him. It might be best if I leave now, before he wakes up again.''

''I don't know to thank you,'' his voice grated.

Kellie swallowed hard. ''Philippe?''

He turned his head in her direction.

''While you tend the baby, why don't I drive Analise home to make sure she gets there safely?''

''I'd like that,'' Analise spoke up before Philippe could answer. ''On the way I'll make a list of do's and don't's for you. Tomorrow I'll phone you to see how things are going.''

Philippe nodded, then flashed Kellie a dark, penetrating glance. ''Drive carefully.''

Once upon a time she would have taken his plea to mean he didn't want anything to happen to her. But things were different now. It was Analise he was worried about.

''I promise.''

Yvette's mother got up from the table. ''Good night, Philippe. Good night, my little one.'' She kissed her grandson's forehead, then followed Kellie out of the dining room.

Neuchâtel was a gentle, beautiful town anytime. At night the lights brought out its elegance. As Kellie drove Analise home, her heart filled to overflowing for this woman who'd turned out to be so generous.

''Analise—''

''You don't have to say anything, my dear. I can see Yvette's baby is in the best of hands.''

''Thank you for what you've done,'' Kellie whispered. ''My husband's a different man tonight.''

''He seems very taken with Jean-Luc. It will be interesting to see how he feels about him by tomorrow evening.''

Kellie sucked in her breath. "I know exactly how he'll feel. He loves him already. That's never going to change."

"Perhaps not. However there might be another reason why he decides not to pursue this any further."

"Why do you say that?" Kellie cried in alarm.

"Because he may discover what I discovered tonight watching the two of them together."

"What are you saying?"

"Yvette convinced me your husband was the father of her baby. Now I'm not so sure."

"You mean because he's not Philippe's exact replica?"

The other woman turned her head toward Kellie. "You noticed it, too. That means your husband will come to the same conclusion if he hasn't done so already."

"But it doesn't necessarily follow they're not father and son. Their coloring's the same. I heard Yvette tell the doctor Philippe was the father. She didn't know I was standing outside the curtain."

"Perhaps my daughter wanted it to be true so badly, it became the truth to her."

Kellie was thankful that Analise's apartment building appeared on the right. She was so shaken by their conversation, she couldn't have driven any further. Pulling over to the curb, she stopped the car.

"Was she seeing another man at the time she met Philippe?"

"Yes. Yvette always had a boyfriend in tow, but no relationship ever turned out to be serious. I hoped she'd end up marrying the new young partner of the veterinarian she worked for.

"They dated quite a bit until she went on her skiing

holiday. But when she returned, she said she'd lost interest in him and found another job. A few months later she broke down and told me she'd met this wonderful man in Chamonix and she was pregnant with his child.

"She refused to reveal his name. I knew nothing until the hospital called and told me she'd been in an accident with Philippe Didier.

"Your husband is an attractive, prominent man whose picture is often in the newspapers showing him out skiing or climbing mountains in the company of Prince Raoul.

"Yvette's infatuation with him was entirely understandable. The fact that she'd been riding with him in his car at the time of the accident seemed proof enough of their past relationship. So naturally when she admitted that he was the father of her baby, I believed her."

"I believed her, too," Kellie's voice throbbed.

Analise expelled a heavy sigh. "If there's any possibility that the baby was fathered by one of her former boyfriends, then we need to find out.

"Why don't you take the baby to Vaudois Hospital for a DNA test tomorrow? Let me know what time your appointment is and I'll meet you there. The sooner we get answers, the better it will be for all of us."

Kellie groaned because everything was much more complicated now. Tonight her husband had fallen in love with a little boy who could be another man's child. If the test wasn't a match, it might not be so easy for Philippe to give him up.

"After what you've just told me, I don't know if it's a good idea for Philippe to spend more time with Jean-Luc until we know."

While they'd been talking, Yvette's mother seemed

to have aged. ''I'm as concerned as you are. After the test is done, I'll take Jean-Luc home with me.''

''If it's possible, I'll get a morning appointment.''

''I'm always home, so the time doesn't matter to me.''

''I'll be sure to bring all the baby's things with us,'' Kellie assured her. But she didn't want to think about tomorrow and how Philippe would feel when Analise went away with him.

''For tonight Jean-Luc will sleep fine in the carryall. So far he's been waking up around one, four and seven for his bottle. He likes it warmed. Other than that, he's been so good I don't have any words of advice.''

The older woman got out of the car. She lowered her head for one last look at Kellie. ''I'll see you tomorrow. If there's a problem at any hour of the night, call me.''

''We will.''

Kellie waited until Analise was safely inside the building, then she headed for the apartment. On the drive back she was plagued by worry.

The older woman's decision to allow the baby an overnight stay meant Philippe wouldn't be going into the office tomorrow. After taking care of the baby all night, what would his mood be like when he had to relinquish Jean-Luc at the hospital?

As she entered the apartment, she expected to see her husband in the living room with the baby. But it appeared he'd taken him to their bedroom. Before starting down the hall, Kellie picked up the carryall.

Philippe had left the door ajar. The light from the bedside lamp revealed his powerful body lounging on top of the bed wearing nothing but the bottom half of a pair of gray sweats. The baby lay across his stomach. Both appeared to be asleep.

The sight of her gorgeous husband with little Jean-Luc touched her deepest emotions.

Yvette's unexpected advent in their lives had represented one nightmare. Now another one was beginning because the baby's paternity was in question.

Not wanting to disturb them, Kellie left the carryall by the door. Knowing she couldn't sleep, she went to the kitchen to do the dishes and clean up the dining room.

Before she prepared for bed, she got the formula out of the diaper bag and put it on the counter ready to warm at a moment's notice. While she worked, she agonized over the fact that she hadn't told Philippe about their baby yet.

But she simply couldn't, not when her husband needed all his powers of concentration to deal with this situation first.

On the brink of emotional and physical exhaustion, she finally went to bed. It seemed like she'd barely closed her eyes when the baby started to cry.

She turned on the lamp and glanced at her watch. It wasn't Jean-Luc's feeding time yet, maybe he was hungry anyway. Throwing on her robe, she hurried down the hall to the master bedroom.

"I'll heat up a bottle," she informed her husband who was bouncing the infant against his shoulder.

In a few minutes it was ready. On her way back to Philippe, she grabbed an ice bag out of the fridge. Once inside the bedroom, she handed him the bottle and a clean cloth. He immediately put the nipple in the baby's mouth. Jean-Luc tugged on it, and quiet reigned.

As Kellie lay the ice bag over his knee, she had to fight not to stare at her husband. Without the beard and moustache, the masculine features she loved so much were visible again. It felt like it had been light years since she'd known the hunger of his kiss. She ached for his touch, for the closeness that might never come again.

"Analise said he should sleep in his carryall. Let me get it."

"What else did you two talk about?" he demanded when she'd brought it to the side of the bed.

She bit her lip, vacillating whether to tell him the truth tonight, or wait until morning.

His dark brows knit together. "Something's going on or she wouldn't have jumped at the chance for a ride home with you."

Nothing escaped his notice. She'd hoped to avoid any serious conversation, but she knew her husband. He wouldn't rest until he had an answer to his question.

Moistening her lips nervously she said, "Analise thinks Yvette may have been lying to her when she claimed you were the father."

He bit out an epithet before raking a free hand through his hair.

"In all fairness to you, she wants to be absolutely certain the baby is yours. She'd like us to take Jean-Luc to the hospital in the morning for a DNA test."

Kellie saw his jaw harden.

"So that's the reason she let him stay over tonight." The fury of his tone tore her apart all over again.

"No, Philippe. You're wrong about that. The thought never crossed her mind that Yvette might have been lying. It wasn't until she watched you interacting earlier that she started to question everything."

"Why?"

"Evidently she couldn't see a strong enough resemblance to be positive you were the father."

He leveled his piercing gaze on her. ''What do *you* see?''

''I—I have to admit he doesn't remind me of you, e-except for his coloring of course. But then a lot of babies don't necessarily look like one of the parents. He could be yours. Did Yvette ever mention another man?''

''I knew nothing about her life.''

''But if you slept with her...''

She watched his chest expand.

''If you had waited for me in the E.R., I would have told you the whole story.''

''I'm here now,'' she said on a ragged breath, sinking down on the end of the bed.

He put the baby against his shoulder to burp him. ''I'd just finished a winter climb with a buddy and was headed back to Neuchâtel. On our way down the mountain we saw evidence of an avalanche. A group of skiers below the ledge were caught in its path. One of them was Yvette.

''When I pulled her out of the snow, she was so frightened and shaken, she begged me to ride with her in the rescue helicopter. At the hospital the doctor checked her out and said she'd be okay. All she needed was warmth and rest.

''I accompanied her back to her hotel room and brought her some dinner. When I told her I had to leave, she broke down sobbing and pled with me to stay.

''Yvette was an attractive thirty-two-year-old woman, but after her near-death experience she seemed so childlike, I felt prompted to hold her for a while so she'd calm down.

''After thanking me over and over again, she finally fell asleep. I had every intention of leaving the room, but I was so exhausted after the climb and rescue effort, I passed out.

"Some time during the night I felt this woman in my arms. She was kissing me and I made the mistake of responding. Before long, the inevitable had happened.

"*Mon Dieu,* I can't begin to describe my self-loathing. I've always detested men who would use a woman like that. I couldn't believe I'd succumbed to a moment of weakness with a literal stranger. Believe me, that's all it was.

"I apologized for my behavior and left the room. After that experience I didn't go near another woman until I met you. As for Yvette, I never saw her again until she came to my work."

The truth was hard to hear, but it was also liberating. Kellie no longer had to fear Yvette's memory because Philippe had never been emotionally involved with her.

"Obviously she didn't have a roommate."

"No. I figured out she'd come alone on her ski trip, probably hoping to meet a man."

Kellie stirred restlessly. "Analise said Yvette had a lot of boyfriends and was dating a veterinarian right up until she left on her holiday. It's possible he might be the baby's father."

"Did she tell you if this man came forward at the funeral asking questions?"

She got up from the bed. "No. The only thing Analise said was that Yvette never got serious over a man until she met you."

He shook his head. "No wonder her hatred of me has been so strong."

"To her credit she let it go, otherwise we wouldn't be lucky enough to have little Jean-Luc with us tonight.

Darling—now that he's fallen asleep, let me put him in his carryall.''

He might as well have not heard her because he held on to the baby. ''If she thinks I'm going to give him back while we wait for the test results, then she's got another think coming.

''In case he's my son, I'll be damned if I'm going to lose out on any more time with him.''

Kellie had known this was going to happen. What Philippe didn't realize was that Analise wouldn't fight him. But the older woman was just as worried as Kellie about the test results.

If they proved he wasn't the father, by then he might feel so attached to the baby, he wouldn't be able to handle losing him. Heaven forbid if Analise found the real birthfather who wanted to claim his son once he learned the truth.

''I know it's late, but could you phone Honore for his advice?''

She waited for her husband to say something. When he didn't dismiss her suggestion out of hand, she realized he was actually considering it.

''I'll phone him now.''

Kellie took that as the signal she should relieve him of the baby. As she walked over to him and reached for Jean-Luc, her arm accidentally brushed against Philippe's hair-roughened chest.

The contact produced a scorching fire. She trembled so hard she almost dropped the baby. Avoiding Philippe's eyes she gathered Jean-Luc against her body like a shield and left the room.

The tiny bundle of warmth provided the distraction she needed. She couldn't make love to her husband, but there was nothing stopping her from kissing Yvette's adorable baby.

He was so sweet she didn't want to put him to bed. Instead she carried him to the living room. After spreading the quilt on the oriental rug, she placed the baby on top of it, then lay down next to him.

Maybe he was dreaming because every once in a while his face made little frowns and his teeny fingers would stretch open, then relax against his receiving blanket.

Could there be any greater preparation for her own baby than to take care of this one? She studied his hands with their miniscule nails which were perfect in every detail down to the half moon cuticles.

When she ran a finger across his lips, his little mouth would form an O. She got the same reaction every time and laughed softly because he was so dear.

No doubt Analise saw Yvette every time she looked at him. Kellie could imagine how empty her house must feel to have her grandson gone tonight.

As she lay there letting the baby hold her little finger in his fist, her mind began to imagine what it would be like if Philippe loved her again and Jean-Luc was theirs. They could buy a home on the outskirts of Neuchâtel with enough bedrooms for several children.

They'd get a dog. She'd plant a garden of flowers and herbs. She would have the kitchen remodeled into her dream kitchen. They'd invite her mother and grandparents to come over and stay for a month or two.

"Wouldn't it be wonderful?" she said to the baby who had opened his eyes and had turned his head in her direction.

"Oh—you're so cute!" She kissed his cheek. It made

him smile. She did it again and again. Finding him irresistible, she picked him up and lifted him in the air.

"What a little angel you are! You haven't cried once for your *grandmère.* How lucky can we be?"

She lowered him to her chest and kissed the top of his head.

"Kellie?"

Philippe had entered the living room without her being aware of it. She had no idea how long he'd been standing there leaning on his cane, but by the tone of his voice something new had upset him.

She drew the baby closer in her arms and got to her feet. Refusing to be intimidated, she faced his unnerving scrutiny without blinking. "Couldn't you reach Honore?"

His eyes narrowed on her features. "We talked."

A burst of adrenaline filled her system. "What's wrong?"

"It's his professional opinion I made a serious mistake the moment I took Analise up on her offer tonight instead of telling her to get an attorney."

"Why?" Kellie blurted. "Isn't it better to settle something like this without having to resort to the law?"

"He believes Yvette and her mother were in on this from the start, that they've always known I wasn't the father."

Oh, no.

"It's the classic story of the girl in trouble. Her mother told her to turn to the man with the most money to bail her out because the birth father had disappeared.

"When the plan went awry and she died a tragic death, the mother didn't want the baby or the financial responsibility. So she laid a guilt trip on me."

Kellie shook her head in despair. ''He's wrong, darling. Totally wrong.''

His face closed up. ''I don't think so. It all fits. After waiting a prolonged period to make the agony worse, she contacted me knowing full well that even if the DNA test proved I wasn't the father, I'd see to the baby's needs.''

His free hand curled into a fist. ''Honore wouldn't be at all surprised if Analise has disappeared by morning, in which case the baby will become a ward of the court until this nightmare can be sorted out.

''Therefore he wants me to take the baby back to her tonight without telling her I'm coming.''

''Phili—''

''I'll need you to drive me,'' he cut in.

Kellie knew what she had to do, but when Philippe heard her confession, there would be repercussions. She didn't want Jean-Luc anywhere around to become upset.

''Give me a second to get his carryall.''

She dashed past him with the baby who was still awake. When she reached the bedroom, she settled him in the carryall and made him comfortable. Then she rummaged in the diaper bag and found the pacifier she'd seen earlier.

He sucked on it the way he did his bottle. She gave him a kiss on his forehead, then got up to leave the room. Philippe was just coming through the door.

Their eyes met for a heartstopping moment. ''Before we do anything, I need to talk to you first. But not in here. Let's go back to the living room where we won't disturb Jean-Luc.''

''Honore said time was of the essence.''

''I—I know something he doesn't.''

A shadow crossed over his face. ''What in the hell does that mean?''

''I'll tell you in the other room.''

She saw no hint of brown in the black eyes impaling her. ''I thought you took longer than usual to do the shopping today.''

He knew.

Her mouth went dry. ''Please can we have this conversation away from the baby?''

CHAPTER SIX

PHILIPPE'S lips twisted unpleasantly. "I think not. Why don't you start by telling me what it was you promised Analise if she would agree to become an entirely different person in the twinkling of an eye?"

Kellie struggled for breath. "Happiness."

In the next instant the cane went crashing against the wall. He took a step forward and seized her shoulders, unaware of his strength.

"Explain that remark."

She didn't care that his grip caused her pain. Kellie had craved his touch for so long, she welcomed any contact with him.

"I told her you needed your son—that if she would give you a chance, her grandchild would grow up to be the luckiest little boy in the world. I promised her she would come to understand why Yvette fell in love with you—why *I* love you so desperately.

"I do love you. More than you'll ever know," she cried before pressing her mouth to his. Out of control at this point, Kellie threw her arms around his neck to draw him closer.

Her desire to know his possession was so great, she could scarcely comprehend it when he wrenched his lips from hers and pushed her away without responding.

Kellie had never known physical rejection from him before. She stepped backward in shock.

Lee's words were screaming in her ears. *Philippe has changed. He wants the divorce now.*

"Forgive me," she whispered in a tortured voice. "That won't happen again."

His eyes held a dangerous glitter. "You're right."

The cryptic remark sent a thrill of alarm through her body. "What do you mean?"

He rubbed his chest absently. "I suppose I ought to thank you for going where the proverbial angels fear to tread. You've served your purpose without my having to take Analise to court. Tomorrow morning you can leave Neuchâtel and we'll call it a day."

His words filled her with panic. "You need me to help with Jean-Luc."

"In the end, Analise has proven to be the best candidate for the job. I need you like I need a steady diet of undetectable poison."

Kellie didn't know he had it in him to be this cruel. His remark might as well have chopped her heart into pieces. She watched him limp the short distance to pick up Jean-Luc who'd started to fuss.

"I know I hurt you terribly when I asked for the divorce. I should never have done it no matter how much I believed I was doing the right thing at the time."

He sat down on the side of the bed with the baby and rubbed his little back until his eyes closed again. Kellie had no way of knowing if her husband was listening or not, but she couldn't stop the words that poured from her heart.

"With hindsight I can see that my behavior didn't have anything to do with loving you. Those selfish actions were all about me. I was still so consumed with pain over being abandoned by my birthfather, I didn't consider what I was doing to you."

Tears stung her eyes. "Darling— I love you. I'd do anything to make our marriage work. Next week I was planning to go for counseling. It's something I should have done as a teenager."

The baby had fallen asleep. Philippe put him back in the carryall before turning to Kellie.

"Are you quite through?"

"No—" At this point her face was dripping with moisture. "I'm begging you for a second chance."

"You mean like the one you gave me when I phoned you a hundred times or more from the hospital?" he fired back.

"Yes! Because you're an honorable man, Philippe. It's one of the things about you I can always count on. You have a nobility that puts you on a different level than most people.

"On the night of the car accident with Yvette, I know for a certainty another man would have done just about anything to keep that kind of truth from his wife.

"Not you!

"You faced me head on, believing our love was strong enough to take it. For that kind of faith and courage, I admire you more than you could possibly imagine.

"I know I don't deserve it, but I'd like to start over again and prove that I can be worthy of you. I swear I'll make a loving home for us. If that includes Jean-Luc, I already adore him. If it doesn't, I'll give you our *own* babies to adore."

By virtue of the fact that she couldn't see any visible signs of emotion, the remote look in his eyes chilled her much more than his anger.

"It's too late for us."

The conviction in his voice shattered her. "Don't say that—"

"I wish I didn't have to. Don't you know I'd sell my soul to feel what I once felt for you?

"Go back to Washington, Kellie. By the end of the week you'll be a free woman. For what it's worth, I hope you get the counseling you need. As for Jean-Luc, I'll take care of him tonight. You need to go to bed. To be frank, you look exhausted. That doesn't augur well for the long flight home."

By some miracle Kellie found the strength to walk to her bedroom and shut the door before collapsing on the bed.

Now you know how Philippe felt when you refused him any opening.

She wanted to die.

As she lay there, she remembered Yvette saying those exact words to the doctor, and his response.

Non, mademoiselle. You want to live. You're going to be a mother very soon. Think of the joy you will have raising your child. I've called your mother. She'll be here shortly to comfort you.

Several hours passed. Kellie heard Philippe in the hall after the baby started to cry for his four o'clock bottle. Then there was silence.

At this point being in the same apartment with him without sharing his life or his bed was unbearable. She dressed and packed. By six o'clock the room and bathroom looked like they'd never been used.

Philippe wanted her gone, so it didn't matter if he could hear her leave. Still, she tried to be as quiet as possible by tiptoeing through their apartment to the front door.

Once she reached the lobby, she used the courtesy phone to ring for a taxi. This early in the morning, the response time was fast. She instructed the chauffeur to drive her to the train station.

As if she were on automatic pilot, she bought a ticket to Nyon on Lake Geneva. According to Lee who had attended a private girls' school in Nyon and had stayed on to work before her marriage, there were dozens of boarding schools dotting the lakeside from Montreux to Geneva. They employed live-in cooks and probably paid well.

Kellie hadn't explored those towns yet. Now that she was on her own, she would get her chance because she had to find a job. The idea of cooking for teenage girls would present a challenge, but that was exactly what Kellie needed to blot out her pain.

She would start by inquiring about a job at Lee's old school. It was an hour away from Neuchâtel. She'd never have to worry about bumping into Philippe.

Once the baby arrived, she'd get word to him. By that time, she would have saved enough money to move back to Neuchâtel and rent a small apartment. Eventually she'd find a woman to tend in the evenings while she worked as a chef.

During the day she would devote all her time to her son or daughter. Philippe would have a lot to say about the way they worked out visitation. That was fine with her. She wanted their child to have a full, rich, loving relationship with its father.

As she stepped off the train in Nyon, her path seemed very clear in her mind. First however, she craved food and a place to lie down where she could sleep off her exhaustion. The hotel across the road from the station would do.

Hours later she lifted her groggy head from the pillow

to glance at her watch. It was already three p.m. She'd been gone from the apartment nine hours.

Had Philippe taken the baby for the test? Was Jean-Luc with him now, or had her husband given him back to Analise because he planned to go to work in the morning?

Kellie would never know the answer to those questions. The pain of her loss was so excruciating, she couldn't imagine getting on with the rest of her life. But she had to!

Before she did anything else she needed to call home. It would be six o'clock on a Monday morning in Eatonville, the one day of the week the restaurant was closed.

Much as she loved her grandparents, she was glad it was her mother who answered.

"Mom?"

"Kellie, honey! I've been so anxious to hear from you. I can tell something's wrong. Is that woman's baby his?"

She sat up in the bed. "He won't know until the DNA tests are completed."

"We're all praying it's another man's child so you and Philippe can get on with your lives."

"That's not going to happen, Mom."

"What do you mean?"

"I did the unforgivable by leaving him at the hospital when he needed me most. It broke up our marriage. He doesn't want me back. We'll be divorced by the end of the week."

"How dare he blame all this on you! Isn't it amazing that a man can sleep around as if it's his divine right, but his sweet little doormat wife better not blink if there are consequences."

"It wasn't like that, Mom, and that isn't the reason why I left."

"After what he did, you're still defending him? Good heavens, Kellie—that man has such a stranglehold on you, he's probably convinced you to forgive your own father."

Kellie took a deep breath. "I *have* forgiven him, Mom. He gave me life, but he didn't have what it took to be a parent. That's why he left. Some people are like that. I know now I had a wonderful life without him. Probably much better."

"I can't believe you just said that."

"It's true. You can't order a person to love you. It has to be a gift. If they can't give it, then you move on."

"Kellie, honey—you don't sound like yourself."

"I think maybe I'm being the real me for the first time in my life."

After a silence, "How soon can we expect you home?"

"I'm not coming home again, except for visits."

"Kellie—"

"I'm staying in Switzerland. Just not with Philippe."

"Why?"

Kellie took a deep breath. Since she'd rushed to Switzerland with Lee, she hadn't had a chance to tell her family about her pregnancy.

"Because I'm having his baby in about seven months."

Her mother gasped. "When did you find out?"

"A few weeks ago."

"Have you seen a doctor?"

"Yes, and everything's fine."

"Don't tell me Philippe is refusing to take care of his pregnant wife!"

"He doesn't know about the baby."

"Oh, Kellie—"

"After it's born, I'll contact him with the news through his attorney. He'll insist on being a vital part of our child's life because that's the kind of man he is. I'll always have to remain close by so we can share in its upbringing."

"Honey—" Her mother's voice cracked.

"It's going to be all right, Mom. Once I find a place to live and get a job, I'll invite you to come for a long visit. Bring Grandma and Grandpa."

"We'll talk about that later. Right now I'm concerned over how you're going to live. You need money."

"I have a little of my own in the bank. It'll be enough until I get my first paycheck."

"I don't want you standing on your feet all day cooking for other people. It's very demanding work and hard on the body. You need to take care of yourself now that you're expecting."

"I know. I'll find something that won't harm me or my baby."

"I could be there tomorrow to help you."

"No, Mom. Much as I appreciate the offer, this is something I have to do myself. I'm a grown woman, and soon to be a mother. It's time I took charge of my life instead of depending on other people."

"But you haven't had enough time to make many friends there yet. You'll be lonely."

Kellie had a true friend in Lee. If an emergency were to arise, she knew she could count on her. As for Raoul, he was too close to Philippe for Kellie to presume on that friendship.

"Once I get a job, that won't be an issue. Mom? Can I ask one favor of you? This goes for the grandparents, too."

"Of course, honey. Anything."

"I know Philippe won't try to contact me again, but you might get phone calls from Claudine or even the Mertiers. If anyone from Europe does ring and asks for me, please don't tell them I haven't returned to Washington.

"Just say that since the divorce, I've been out looking for a good job. It won't be a lie. Take the message and tell them I'll get in touch with them at the first opportunity."

There was a long silence. "We'll keep your secret, but Kellie— I expect you to call every few days so I know you're all right. Otherwise I won't have a moment's peace."

"I promise, Mom. I love you. Give Grandma and Grandpa a kiss for me."

She hung up the phone, relieved to know that Claudine, particularly, would never find out Kellie was still in Switzerland. Much as she loved Philippe's sister, it was better that she remain uninformed so she couldn't let something slip in her brother's company.

Having made contact with home, Kellie could get ready to apply for a job. In order to make the right impression, she put on her navy blazer with matching skirt, and wore her hair up with a tortoiseshell clip.

Later, as the taxi drove her through the charming little town full of Roman artifacts and history, she could see why Lee had loved working here. Kellie should be so lucky.

As they entered the private gravel driveway, the school turned out to be an imposing French manor house surrounded by a wooded estate facing the water.

Kellie paid the chauffeur and hurried up the steps to the main doors of the school. A uniformed maid answered the buzzer. When Kellie said she wanted to the see the headmistress, she was shown into an elegant salon and told to wait.

Ten minutes later, when she was sure she'd been forgotten, a stylish looking woman of seventy-five years or so came in the room. Kellie stood up.

"I'm Madame Simoness. You wanted to see me?" the headmistress asked in French.

"Yes, *madame,*" she answered in kind. "My name is Kellie Madsen." She didn't dare say Didier. Philippe's name was known everywhere. "I'm looking for a temporary job."

The older woman shook her gray head. "I'm sorry. If you were thinking of a teaching position, we're fully staffed and only hire native French speakers from our local universities."

"I should have said I'm a chef. I've worked in my grandfather's restaurant business since I was a little girl. After I obtained my B.A. in French, I went on to train as a French chef at the Maison Pierre Institute in Napa Valley, California.

"I lived in Paris, married a Frenchman and moved to Neuchâtel with him, but it didn't last. I would like to stay on here and work until my baby is born. I enjoy being around teens, and a boarding school would be a lovely change from a public restaurant."

After Kellie's long speech, Madame Simoness laughed. "Your credentials sound impressive, but you've impressed me much more by being forthright. How did you happen to hear about Beau Lac?"

"The newspapers were filled with the modern day fairy tale of Prince Raoul's marriage to the American. Several articles mentioned that she'd been a student here, and was even on your staff for a while. It caught my attention."

A pair of shrewd eyes stared at Kellie for a long moment. "Let me think about it. Before you go, step into my office next door. My secretary will give you a form to fill out. Leave a phone number where I can reach you."

"In the morning I'll be taking a train to Lausanne to do some more interviews. Would it be all right if I call you from there, say tomorrow afternoon around tea time?"

"That will be fine."

"Thank you, *madame.*"

Midafternoon a local fisherman dropped off a fresh catch of whitefish from the lake for the girls' Friday night grand diner. Kellie had just started to prepare it when she heard the secretary call to her from the kitchen doorway.

"Yes, Francoise?"

"Madame Simoness says there's a Monsieur Dufont waiting for you in the petit salon."

Honore?

The knife fell out of her hand.

Her mother had promised to keep her whereabouts a secret. The fact that he'd come here in person could only mean one thing...

She started to shake and couldn't stop.

"Thank you, Francoise. I'll be right there."

The other cook filling the individual pots with spinach soufflé looked over at her. "Take all the time you need. I'll finish the fish."

"You're an angel, Lucie."

Kellie removed her apron, washed her hands a couple of times, then ran through the huge manor house forgetting she was pregnant. Her hand fairly shook as she turned the handle of the door to the salon.

"Honore?" she cried. "It's Philippe, isn't it? Something's happened to him!"

"Kellie—" The patrician-looking attorney with the salt and pepper hair reached for her and gave her hug.

"If your husband were in the hospital, your mother would have told you before I could get here," he assured her, giving her a kiss on both cheeks. "But he needs your help if you're willing to give it."

Faint with relief, other emotions quickly took over. "I'm not his wife anymore," she moaned the words in agony. "He doesn't want any part of me, Honore. You above all people know that."

"A great deal has happened while you've been out of touch. As soon as you can get ready, we'll drive to Neuchâtel. There isn't a moment to lose."

"But my job—"

"The headmistress has already given her permission for you to leave," he interjected. "She understands this is an emergency."

Honore could move mountains.

"Just tell me one thing. Did Philippe ask you to talk to me?"

"No. This is all my idea."

The pieces of her broken heart shriveled up inside her. "He'll never believe I didn't use you to see him again. I—I can't come with you."

"After you ran away the first time, I thought you'd learned your lesson."

He'd said the words in a gentle tone, but she felt their sting.

"Exercise your faith and trust me. All will be revealed in good time."

A shudder ran through her body. "Give me a few minutes and I'll meet you at the car."

An hour later they'd reached Philippe's office. Honore had been in contact with Marcel to make certain his boss would be alone by the time they arrived.

Kellie couldn't imagine what Honore was up to. All she had to go on was his affection for her husband. "I'm frightened."

"You leave everything to me. Come on, let's go in."

The excitement of seeing Philippe again warred with her fear that he'd take one look at her and tell her to go back where she came from.

When Marcel saw Kellie enter Philippe's suite with Honore, he did a double take. But that didn't prevent him from getting up to greet her with a kiss on both cheeks. "It's good to see you again, Kellie."

"Thank you. It's nice to see you too."

His questioning gaze darted to Honore. "Shall I tell him you're here?"

"That's all right. You go on home."

"Good night then."

As Honore knocked on the inner door, Kellie's heart leaped to her throat.

"Come in."

When they entered, Philippe was turned to the side of his desk studying something on the computer screen. He didn't immediately look up. It gave Kellie a moment to drink in the sight of her husband whose dark, handsome looks would always thrill her.

He wore his gray silk suit, the one she'd given him for a birthday present. Evidently he'd put the past so completely behind him, he could wear it without remembering their night of passion on his boat. The one he kept tied up at Raoul's private pier.

She'd planned a private birthday celebration. Afterward they'd taken a midnight ride on the lake and had ended up making love until morning. Was it possible to forget a memory like that? her heart cried.

The two of them sat down on the chairs opposite Philippe's desk. He'd had a haircut since she'd last seen him. There was no more sign of weight loss, but he hadn't gained any, either.

"One minute, Marcel."

"Take your time," Honore answered.

Philippe's head swiveled around. His penetrating black gaze fused with Kellie's in stunned surprise.

"*Mon Dieu,* what are you doing here?" He sounded more haunted than angry.

"She came with me when I told her you were in for the fight of your life if you hoped to gain custody of Jean-Luc. What she doesn't know is that the DNA test proved that Dr. Bruchard, the veterinarian, is the baby's birth father."

"What?" Kellie blurted helplessly.

Philippe seemed to have a struggle dragging his eyes from her to look at Honore.

"We've been over this before. It would be a long shot now, even if I had a wife." Philippe sounded like he'd had all he could take.

Honore eyed him directly. "In anticipation of a custody battle, I never filed the divorce papers you signed. You and Kellie are still legally married."

Kellie gasped, then looked away, afraid to see the shock and displeasure in her husband's eyes.

Philippe suddenly got to his feet and moved around the desk. She noticed he was walking without a limp or his cane, reminding her of the old Philippe who was once again in total control of his life. His narrowed gaze flicked from Honore to Kellie.

"You're actually willing to go through a court case that will be in all the papers, knowing nothing will probably come of it except more notoriety?"

"Of course," she cried softly. *Don't you understand this is the second chance I've been praying for?* "I know how much you love that baby. If you don't win the case, at least you'll have the peace of mind knowing you did everything you could."

He seemed in the grip of some unnamed emotion. Kellie watched his broad chest rise and fall several times. Her breathing was just as shallow. She couldn't believe that a few hours ago she'd been miles away cutting up fish, and now...

Honore patted Philippe's arm. "While you two sort things out, I'm going to fly back to Paris. I have an early-morning appointment. We'll keep in close touch. I'll get the earliest court date I can."

He kissed her cheek and disappeared, leaving a trembling Kellie standing close enough to her husband, she could feel his warmth.

Philippe's eyes played over her for an unsettling moment. "I'll drive you to the apartment. You must be hungry and tired after your long flight."

Actually she was neither one. Being with him again had brought her to glorious life. As for her appetite, since she'd taken Dr. Cutler's advice by eating carrot and celery sticks between meals, she wasn't starving all the time.

The hard part now was telling her husband as much of the truth as he she thought he could handle.

"There was no plane trip, Philippe."

His dark brows knit together. "You weren't in Washington when Honore phoned you?"

"No." She could feel her heart rate picking up speed. "After I left the apartment, I made the decision to stay in Switzerland."

His head reared.

"Not with the Mertiers," she blurted before he could accuse her of using his good friends.

He rubbed the back of his neck in a gesture he probably wasn't aware of whenever he pondered something serious. "Where have you been all this time?"

"Earning my living as a cook at Beau Lac in Nyon."

Her husband didn't move a muscle. In fact it was his very stillness that let her know she'd shocked him once again.

"In case you're worried I dropped Lee's name or yours to influence the headmistress, you couldn't be more wrong. I applied as Kellie Madsen, divorcée, and let my credentials speak for me."

Their eyes held. "Do you live there?" his voice grated.

"Yes. Madame Simoness is a terrific person to work for. Another woman and I share the cooking. I was preparing fish for dinner when the secretary told me I had a visitor.

"Obviously Honore had phoned my mother and she told him where I was. He obtained Madame's permission for me to leave before I even knew about it."

Something flashed in the dark recesses of his eyes. "Is this the truth?"

"Smell my hands."

When she lifted them, he grabbed hold of her wrists and inhaled. She saw him stare at her ringless fingers before relinquishing them. *What she'd give to be wearing his wedding ring again.*

"Why, Kellie?" he whispered, still incredulous.

"Because I don't feel that Washington is my home anymore. I love Switzerland. I thought if I could find a place where you would never have to see me or know I was around, it would be all right." It was impossible to swallow. "Are you very angry?"

"*Mon Dieu,* what a question!"

She averted her eyes. "You weren't supposed to find out. The thing is, Lucie, the other cook, is teaching me Swiss cuisine. It's an invaluable experience. As for the girls, they're wonderful and my French is improving every day.

"However, my job at Beau Lac is only temporary. I was planning to leave there when school is out. But if Nyon is too close for you, I'll tell Madame and find employment farther away."

His hands had gone to his hips in a totally masculine stance. With such an incredibly attractive husband, it was hard to concentrate on anything but him.

"If we're going to be a credible couple throughout this custody suit, we'll be too busy for you to work."

"Has Analise let you keep Jean-Luc all this time?"

He seemed to be concentrating on her mouth. For the first time since she'd returned from Washington, she felt he was actually looking at her and not through her.

"No. When we met at the hospital, she said she'd contacted the man Yvette had been dating before she left on her ski trip. The moment she asked him if could have been the father of her baby, he said yes and asked to see Jean-Luc.

"Analise hadn't expected that response. Once he visited her apartment, he went for a DNA test. She felt it might be better for everyone if there was no visitation until we knew the results."

"I'm sorry, Philippe. That couldn't have been easy."

"It wasn't. Now things are worse because he knows he's the father. He says he wants his son."

"Does Analise feel he's sincere?"

"She doesn't know what to think. He's not married and is struggling to get his career going. But he *is* Jean-Luc's rightful father. I'm not sure I have a case."

"As long as there's any chance at all, we have to take it!" Her declaration bounced off the walls.

"Then you'll have to give up your job."

"How soon do you want me to tell Madame Simoness?"

"Tonight."

Much as she hated to put out the headmistress, this was Kellie's husband asking for her help. It was her last chance to try and save their marriage.

"I'll phone her now."

"Tell her we're going house hunting this weekend."

"We are?" *Maybe she was dreaming.*

"The court will send out someone from social services to see what kind of a home we can provide for Jean-Luc. The company apartment is no place to rear a child. We'll need to find a property with separate living quarters in anticipation of the day we break in a nanny."

Kellie turned away from him in desolation.

CHAPTER SEVEN

PHILIPPE had changed during the three weeks Kellie had worked at Beau Lac. All that bitter anger and contempt for her seemed to be missing.

In their place a new Philippe had been resurrected. He treated her with courtesy and respect, the way he would an acquaintance or a client visiting the show room. But it was as if he had no emotions beneath the surface.

After two days of looking at houses with him, she thought she preferred the first version. At least his rage had meant he was alive with feelings.

She darted him a sideward glance. He appeared relaxed as he drove them from one property to another where the realtor waited for them each time. Watching him walk up and down stairs, climb in and out of the car, shift gears, you'd never know he'd suffered a knee injury, thank heaven.

To her chagrin he caught her looking at him. "What did you think of the last place?"

She wondered what kind of reaction she'd get if she told him any one of the twenty plus chalet-type houses they'd seen was fine with her. Nothing mattered when she knew he was counting the days until they broke in a nanny and he no longer needed Kellie in his life.

"It was lovely. They all are. If you have strong feelings about one of them, that will be fine with me." The choice of house didn't matter because she didn't dare get attached to anything.

If he lost the suit—a possibility they had to face—she'd be out on her own again much sooner anyway. Hopefully before she began to show.

Though her clothes were starting to fit tighter around the waist, she didn't think she'd start to look pregnant for another couple of months.

She was grateful that she didn't suffer from morning sickness. Except for being more tired than usual, she felt fine and had gotten her eating habits under control.

If she were careful to wear loose fitting outfits, Philippe wouldn't notice the difference. For that to happen he would have to be intimate with her to detect the changes to her body. To her devastation, sending him those divorce papers had killed his desire for her.

"There's one more house on the list the realtor wants to show us. After that we'll stop for an early dinner somewhere and make a firm decision on one of them."

She noticed he'd headed for the lake road. After a few minutes they passed the private entrance to the fabulous Château D'Arillac where she'd stayed with Raoul and Lee part of the day.

Kellie would have loved to see them again. Unfortunately that wasn't going to happen, either. Philippe might not bring it up, but he would never forgive her for using the Mertiers to help her reunite with him at their chalet in Zermatt.

She feared it would make no difference to Philippe that at Raoul's urging, Lee had flown all the way to Washington to take Kellie back to Switzerland. He would blame her for not finding another way to approach him once she'd arrived in Neuchâtel. One that didn't involve his friends.

The idea that there might be a possible rift between

Philippe and Raoul because he'd helped Kellie only added to her pain.

Grieving for all that might have been if she hadn't deserted Philippe at the hospital, she didn't realize they'd arrived at the next property until he'd stopped the car. The realtor had arrived ahead of them.

One look through the chestnut trees shading a small, charming nineteenth century château and Kellie let out a cry of uninhibited delight.

"Finally a reaction," Philippe murmured before getting out of the car to help her.

"It's looks like something right out of the Loire Valley."

During her stay with the Didiers in Paris, Philippe had taken her to visit the French château country. It had been a time of pure enchantment.

Their realtor checked his watch. "I have some phone calls to make. Why don't I let you two take a look around. I'll be right here if you want to go inside."

Kellie was glad he'd offered to leave them alone for a change.

When they walked to the front part facing the lake, she came to a standstill. "Oh, look! There's a tower on the end. I can just see Jean-Luc and his friends using it to play knights."

A trace of a smile hovered around her husband's lips. His reaction spoke volumes. For over a month Philippe had believed Jean-Luc was his little boy.

If you think you love him, my darling, wait until our own little child makes its arrival.

"Let's keep walking, shall we?"

She agreed to his suggestion, not needing any urging.

Lawn covered a portion of the grounds. But mostly

it was woodsy. Through the trees she saw a dock for Philippe's boat.

When they reached the back, another surprise greeted her. There was a plot of ground which had once been a garden. Next to it stood an empty greenhouse.

With all the overgrown foliage, it was evident this part of the property had been neglected for years. In her mind's eye she could imagine how beautiful everything would have looked in its prime.

There was a gravel driveway leading to the greenhouse. They followed it around to the area where they'd parked the car. Tucked off in the trees, almost out of sight, was a garage.

"Do you want to go inside the château?" Philippe asked in a quiet aside.

"If you would," she whispered back, trying not to show her excitement.

He nodded to the agent who let them in through the front door. There was a large entrance hall with a graceful, curving stairway. It led to the second floor where there were five bedrooms, each with their own bathrooms.

The main floor contained a living room, a smaller sitting room, another room that could be a library or a music room, a dining room, kitchen, bathroom, pantry and wine cellar.

Kellie adored the interior on sight because of the many windows and the amount of light they let in.

"This is a very gracious château, built on a small scale so as not to be unmanageable for the modern day family. The tower is its own apartment."

One mention of it and Kellie suffered more anguish knowing Philippe would be willing to buy it for that aspect alone.

She could see dollar signs in the realtor's eyes. No doubt this property had been on the market for a while. It would take a fortune to renovate.

Only someone with Philippe's kind of money could afford to purchase such an estate and the realtor knew it. Kellie wasn't going to let the man get away with robbery if she could help it.

"It is charming, but the place has been neglected and needs a lot of work." The outside more than the interior, but he didn't need to know that. "Thank you so much for your time, Monsieur Penot." She turned to Philippe. "I'll see you at the car."

On that note she left the house. It wasn't long before both men followed. She heard her husband say goodbye to the realtor before he opened the door and climbed in the driver's seat.

When he joined her, he didn't immediately start the engine. "You loved this house the minute you saw it, so what was all that about?"

"I didn't want the realtor to think I preferred it over the others for fear he'd charge you an even more exorbitant price."

An amused expression crossed over his face. She hadn't seen that look for so long she thought maybe she needed glasses.

"I appreciate your being mindful of my interests. As it happens, I'm very taken with this place myself. It appears we've come to the end of our search."

With that separate apartment, Kellie knew why!

"Under the circumstances I think we'll let Monsieur Penot worry about making a sale until tomorrow, then I'll call him with an offer. If your tactics worked, he won't counter."

On that note he started the car. "Where would you like to eat?"

Their honeymoon marriage had been over for weeks. She couldn't bear to go out in public with him and pretend they were a happy couple when in reality he would be getting rid of her at the first opportunity.

"Why don't you call one of your friends and enjoy dinner out while I drive to Nyon? Madame Simoness was very gracious about everything over the phone, but I'd like to say a proper goodbye to her and pick up my things."

The amused look faded. "I'd intended to drive you there on another day and give her my personal thanks as well. If you're that anxious to see her, we'll go together now."

He put the car in gear and they were off. En route he stopped at a corner market and came back out loaded with meat pies, a baguette, cheese, chocolate and her favorite grape juice drink.

It was like the old days when they went for rides through the Swiss countryside. Except that he was no longer her lover. She didn't feed him while he drove. She didn't laugh with lovelight in her eyes when he pretended to nibble on her fingers.

There were no stolen kisses or whispers of endearment. No intimacy. He didn't run his hand through her hair or caress her thigh as a prelude to making love.

Those days were gone.

How foolish of her to have turned down dinner. She'd thought going out with him would be too painful. But being in the close confines of the car with him like this brought back too many haunting memories. It was torture not being able to kiss him and touch him whenever she felt like it.

They arrived at Beau Lac in record time. While Kellie dashed off to get the few things she'd left in her room, Philippe talked privately with the headmistress.

Afterward she joined them to give the older woman an affectionate hug goodbye. With the promise that she'd stay in touch, Kellie went out to the car with Philippe. He stashed her belongings in the back seat.

"Would you like to hear what she had to say about you?" he asked once they'd started down the driveway.

"Madame Simoness isn't that crazy about Americans, so I can imagine."

"After the untimely death of her husband forty years ago, she started the school. Since then she has seen dozens of excellent cooks come and go, but none of them ever served meals like yours, or made such a favorable impact on the girls."

Kellie's face went hot at the unexpected compliment. "That was very nice of her. I'm sure she was exaggerating."

He flashed her a dark, penetrating glance. "On the contrary. She didn't want to let you go. Before you came back to the office, she had just guaranteed you a salary they're paying world class chefs these days if you would consider staying on."

"I'm very flattered," she said in a quiet voice.

Madame Simoness was kindness itself. She knew about Kellie's plight. It was her way of letting Kellie know she could have a permanent position with her after the baby was born. If Beau Lac were located in Neuchâtel, Kellie would take her up on it in a heart beat. But the baby's happiness had to come above all other considerations.

The problems of arranging visitation were bad enough when divorced parents lived in the same city.

To have to travel for an hour to be with your child was ludicrous. She couldn't do that to Philippe or their baby.

"I told you what she said because I think it only fair to warn you I'll probably lose the custody suit. Since you told me you wanted to stay in Switzerland, I would hate to see you pass up such a rare opportunity. Beau Lac is this country's most prestigious private school."

At his words, her heart almost failed her.

Was he so anxious to get rid of her, he was willing to forego the court battle? But how could that be when he'd just decided on a house in which to raise Jean-Luc if he won?

Philippe, my love— What's going on inside of you?

"I—I agree it's a generous offer. But I'm committed to helping you. When the time comes for me to look for work again, I'll find something else I like."

"Why don't you sleep on it."

"I don't need to!" she fired back, crushed by his eagerness to see the last of her.

"That sounded final."

Again she thought she heard an element of levity in his tone. She simply didn't understand him.

"It *was* final."

"Because you'd rather run your own restaurant."

"Well, yes...someday." But with a baby coming, she couldn't see that dream coming to fruition in the near future. Maybe never.

They rode the rest of the distance to the apartment in silence. Philippe's thoughts seemed to be as ponderous as hers. Glad that they had arrived, she disappeared into the guest room like a good little girl and got ready for bed.

After brushing her teeth, she reached for the bottle of prenatal vitamins Dr. Cutler had given her. She'd kept it hidden in a satin hose bag in her drawer so Philippe wouldn't find it.

To her shock she discovered there were only five pills left. She needed to make an appointment with an obstetrician right away. Maybe Lee knew someone who could recommend a good one.

After Philippe left for work in the morning, she'd give her a call. Close to a month had gone by without hearing a word from her or Raoul. Kellie desperately needed a good friend to talk to in private. Someone she could trust.

No one filled that role better than the princess, a new bride who had left her real-life prince right after their honeymoon to help reunite Philippe and Kellie. That kind of selflessness was humbling. She owed them so much.

Depending on Lee's schedule, maybe she'd be able to come to the apartment for lunch. On the plane Kellie had learned that Lee loved authentic Mexican food. It was the one thing she missed about living in Europe.

If Kellie got busy shopping early, she could surprise her with homemade chili verde burritos, guacamole and refried beans.

Hoping against hope Lee would be home in the morning, Kellie turned out the light and slid beneath the covers. After so much agony of spirit, a visit with her would be a high point.

She'd just closed her eyes when she heard a rap on the door. "Kellie?"

Her pulse went crazy. "I—I'm awake. Come in."

As he pushed it open, she saw his silhouette outlined by the hall light. He was wearing his favorite blue robe. More often than not she'd ended up putting it on to bring him breakfast in bed after a night of making love.

If he'd worn it to torture her with what might have been if she hadn't destroyed their marriage, it was a cruel trick.

"I've just told Marcel I'm taking the next two weeks off from work so we can get the house ready to move in. As soon as I phone Monsieur Penot in the morning and get the keys, I thought we'd spend the day out there. We'll need to make a list of things that need doing immediately."

A whole day with Philippe at their future home, no matter how temporary, filled her with too much excitement. Inviting Lee for lunch would have to be put off for a while longer, but she would still need to call her about a doctor.

"Do you want me to pack a lunch?"

"Why don't we pick up some food on the way? I'll drive the boat over to our dock. If it needs some repairs, we'll find out. When we get hungry, we'll go out on the lake to eat. The good weather we've been having ought to hold, so it should be warm enough."

"That sounds wonderful," she said with a tremor in her voice.

"I'd like to get started early. Can you be ready by eight?"

"Of course."

She felt him hesitate.

"Kellie?"

"Yes?"

"I intend to compensate you for your sacrifice for Jean-Luc."

I don't want compensation— I just want my husband back, she cried inwardly.

"It's no sacrifice, Philippe."

There's nothing I'd love more than to mother that precious little boy.

With the light at his back, she couldn't see his expression.

"Don't forget the statistics are against the judge ruling in my favor."

Her eyes closed tightly. "I can still hope for a miracle."

"We'll see," he whispered. "Good night." He shut the door, enclosing her in darkness.

She set her alarm for seven. To her surprise she slept surprisingly well. When it went off, she showered and dressed in a pair of jeans she'd bought in Nyon.

They were a larger size to accommodate her changing dimensions. Paired with a loose fitting navy pullover and sneakers, she would be totally comfortable all day.

By the time Philippe walked in the kitchen similarly dressed, she had breakfast ready on the counter. He reached for a warm brioche and finished it off in two bites.

"The house is now in the Didier name." There was a ring of satisfaction in his voice.

She darted him a brief glance, hungry for the sight of her husband who was so attractive, he made all the senses in her body come alive.

"For how much?"

There was an odd gleam in his eyes as they swept over her. "Let's just say I have no complaints. He'll meet us there with the keys in half an hour."

"Then we'd better hurry."

She poured yogurt on her bowl of cereal and bananas. Philippe liked his with milk. When they were through eating, he finished off with a cup of coffee.

"You want me to pour you some?"

Caffeine could be bad for the baby. ''No, thank you. When I planned the menus for the girls, I told them they were going to eat healthy. Above all no more wine or stimulants. That meant I had to be a role model. After three weeks abstinence, I'm out of the habit of drinking tea, coffee or wine. I feel so much better, I hope to cut them from my diet permanently.''

''That's very commendable, but I'm surprised they didn't go on strike,'' he drawled, reminding her of the man she'd fallen in love with.

''I substituted orange juice and milk. Skim, of course, but they didn't know it. For dinner they could have ice water. That was a hit with everyone except the Americans.''

Philippe chuckled. ''Do I dare ask what you served them for tea?''

Her lips curved upward. ''Well, I did away with the pastries. They could have water and all the raw vegetables they could eat.''

By now his chuckles had become full blown laughter. It was a glorious sound she hadn't heard for so long, it warmed her all the way to the car.

Once they were on their way to the house, he said, ''Obviously it was your meals that saved you from annihilation.''

She gave her husband a covert glance. For a little while she felt like they'd gone back to those euphoric days of their marriage before she'd ever heard of Yvette. If only this laughter and sharing would go on and on until that wall of ice around his heart thawed completely!

When they reached the house, Mr. Penot was waiting for them with a smile on his face. He walked toward the car and opened the door for her.

"*Bonjour, madame.*"

"Good morning, Monsieur."

"Congratulations on your beautiful purchase. I hope you will be very happy here."

Kellie was afraid that would require a miracle.

"Thank you for showing it to us."

"You're welcome. I have all the keys in this envelope." He handed it to her. "They're labeled. If you have any problem, don't hesitate to phone."

Philippe walked around to shake his hand. They chatted amicably in the brisk November air for a moment before the other man got in his car and left for another appointment.

But just as she'd feared, when her husband turned to her, all signs of laughter had left his striking features. The little interlude allowing her a glimpse of past joy was nothing more than an aberration.

"Since we didn't see the tower yesterday, let's start there first."

Steeling herself not to feel pain, she accompanied him across the lawn where the early rays of the sun dappled through the trees onto the creamy stone exterior of the château. The effect was breathtaking.

If Philippe was thinking the same thing, he didn't bother to tell her. By the time they'd reached the door of the tower, she'd found the key. After turning it several ways, it finally clicked. Philippe pushed it open.

They entered a perfectly circular room with hardwood floors, a fireplace and a bathroom. A deep rectangular window that looked out toward the woods filled the room with light.

Enchanted, she hurried up the steps of the yellow stone staircase mellowed with age. The top floor was identical to the other, but there was no fireplace or bathroom.

Kellie ran over to the window and opened it. She could see beyond the trees to the jewel-like lake. There were clusters of chalets dotting the lush green landscape. To be a child in this house would be like living in fairyland.

"What do you think?" sounded a deep male voice directly behind her.

Philippe's proximity made her tremble. She closed the window. "The nanny won't ever want to leave the tower. What we have to do now is choose which room in the house will make the best nursery."

She slipped past him and practically ran down the flight of stairs. Once she was outside, she searched in the envelope for the key to the front door. Philippe caught up with her at the main entrance.

Avoiding his eyes, she turned the key to the left. It was a lucky guess. The door opened without problem.

The main house contained honey-toned inlaid wood floors of nineteenth century design. Again she was impressed by the play of light giving everything a dreamy quality.

Without waiting for her husband, she rushed up the stairs. The double doors at the head of the staircase led to the master bedroom with its fireplace. Two bedrooms flanked either side. All the bedrooms had been papered in nineteenth century prints which looked worn and faded.

As she entered the first one on the right she said, "Whoever designed this house didn't believe in children being accessible to the parents. If this is where you're going to put Jean-Luc, there ought to be a connecting door to your bedroom."

"That can be done easily enough. Do you have any idea about the decor?"

"I've seen pictures of matching window shades and ceiling trims for children that would be adorable in here. But the wallpaper would need to be removed. If we painted the walls an off-white and bought an area rug to match the trim, then we could buy baby furniture to decorate around it.

"For that matter it wouldn't hurt to remove all the paper in the house and paint everything the same color. It will make it smell fresh. Later on you can go with any kind of decor you want.

"My taste is eclectic. I like to mix periods and colors. However you might want to replicate what has been removed."

"Everything you've suggested makes perfect sense. Let's inspect the kitchen."

Kellie already knew she loved it and told him so once they'd checked the appliances and cupboards. "This is the heart of the home. It needs a good professional cleaning, and there might be some plumbing problems down the road, but I wouldn't change anything else about it."

"You're the expert here," he murmured.

"Maybe, but I wouldn't have a clue where to start with the grounds."

"That's easy. I'll get some gardeners to cut everything back so we can see the original design of the landscaping."

She wandered over to the French doors that led to the empty greenhouse. The place reminded her of Malmaison outside Paris, another spot where Philippe had taken her. As they'd sauntered around the estate, she'd been so in love with him, it had hardly registered they were looking at the greenhouse where the Empress Josephine once grew exotic plants.

Kellie pressed her head against the glass. Too many memories were suffocating her. She'd thought she could help Philippe. She'd thought she could do this, but every minute with him was tearing her apart a little more.

"It's almost lunchtime. Do you want to go with me to get the food?"

She refused to look at him. "If you don't mind, I'd like to stay here and explore some more."

After a brief silence, "Suit yourself. I'll bring our meal back in the boat. Meet me at the pier in about a half hour."

It was on the tip of her tongue to ask him to leave his cell phone. But then he'd wonder who she was calling. At this point it looked like she'd have to wait until they got back to the apartment before she could phone Lee.

With the whole house to herself she had the luxury of imagining her own child running through these rooms, playing on the stairs. A little boy or girl who would have inherited certain attributes of Philippe like his piercing dark eyes, his enticing smile, his lean, powerful build, his black hair, his beautiful olive complexion.

Her hand went to her belly. The baby inside her so snug and tight would belong here. In time it would follow its daddy around with a worshipful expression.

Would their child grow up to love mountain climbing? Fast ca—

"Kellie? Are you in here?"

It was a woman's voice calling to her with a distinct American accent.

"Lee?"

"Yes!"

She fairly flew through the common rooms to the foyer. "I can't believe it! I was going to call you today."

They started toward each other at the same time and hugged. "You don't know how many times Raoul and I wanted to find out what was going on, but we didn't dare interfere."

"You mean Philippe hasn't tried to get in touch with him?"

"Your husband hasn't phoned any of his friends."

"Then how did you know I was here?"

"Raoul was on his way to town and happened to pass Philippe on the lake road. One thing led to another. He just phoned me and told me to drive over here. We're going to have lunch with you out in the boat. I hope that's all right." Her violet eyes searched Kellie's for approval.

"Oh, Lee, it's more than all right! It means they can go back to being friends again!" She hugged her once more.

"So can we!" Lee asserted.

"Every day I've wanted to call you, but Philippe was so angry about my being at the chalet, I was afraid to contact you."

"Before I hear all the details, just tell me one thing—"

Kellie could read her mind. "He doesn't know about the baby yet. I'm only here on sufferance to help him win custody of Jean-Luc. If he gets him, then Philippe expects me to break in a nanny before I leave. Naturally if he doesn't win custody, then I'm to go."

Lee stared hard at her. "The point is, you're still

here. When you consider his state of mind after you left the hospital, that has to mean something.''

''I wish it were true,'' she half-sobbed. ''Lee—while we're still alone I have something important to ask you. Could you help me find a good obstetrician here in Neuchâtel?''

''You can go to mine,'' she said poker faced. But her eyes held a glow that gave her secret away.

''*You're* pregnant?''

''Yes!''

Kellie hugged her again. ''Does Raoul know?''

''No. I only found out yesterday afternoon. He was in Geneva until late, so I was putting off telling him until tonight.''

''To think you're going to have a little prince or princess. Your husband will be the happiest man alive. When are you due?''

''June.''

''Our children will only be about a month apart.''

''Kellie?'' She said after handing her the doctor's card from her purse. ''Why don't you tell Philippe the truth now?''

''Because the custody suit's coming up. I don't want to upset him anymore than he already is. You don't know what he's been like.''

''Tell me.''

Relieved to have a close friend to talk to, Kellie began at the beginning. When she'd finished, Lee stood there shaking her head.

''Madame Simoness is a wonderful person to turn to in times of trouble, but why didn't you phone me? You could have stayed with us.''

''Oh, no, I couldn't. Philippe would never have forgiven me.''

"Well he can't keep us apart now. If you had any idea how much Raoul has missed your husband..."

Tears filled Kellie's eyes. "I've missed him, too."

While she was brushing the moisture away, they both heard the blare of a horn. It was coming from the boat.

Lee turned her silvery-blond head to Kellie. "They're pulled up to the pier, and we're all together. You can't tell me this isn't a good omen."

CHAPTER EIGHT

KELLIE wasn't a person to believe in omens, but if she could be thankful for one thing, Philippe seemed to have accepted the Mertiers back in his life.

He didn't fool Kellie. Her husband would never have bought a home so close to Raoul if it hadn't been what he'd wanted all along.

Over the next two weeks they were constant visitors. Raoul appeared to have put his princely duties on hold. While Kellie and Lee supervised the workmen indoors, their husbands cleared away the undergrowth outside right along with the gardeners.

Though Raoul tried to soft-pedal it around Philippe, the knowledge that he was going to be a father had put a new light in his eyes. Kellie was so happy for them.

Lee was a constant delight. Like Kellie, she was more modern in her tastes. After living at the centuries old Château D'Arillac, she thought Kellie's ideas to mix and match provided the ideal compromise between present and past.

When they were finished with the house, Kellie had promised to help Lee. She and her husband were planning to remodel a room in their private apartment at the château into a nursery.

During one of their many shopping expeditions to town, Kellie was able to meet with Dr. Loubel, Lee's O.B. He reminded her a lot of her old family doctor and couldn't have been nicer. Evidently her pregnancy was coming along fine. He gave her a supply of vitamins and said he'd see her the next month.

As the days went by, more and more furnishings were delivered to the house. Except for a few pieces of furniture and pictures brought from the company apartment, they'd bought everything else new.

One afternoon while Kellie was fastening a mobile to the baby's crib, Philippe made an appearance. He had that dark, brooding expression on his face she hadn't seen for a while. It killed her when he looked like that.

"What's wrong?"

"We have a visitor downstairs."

"Who is it?"

"Madame Frouneau, the social worker from the court."

This was what Kellie was really here for. To help him win his suit.

"Then aren't we lucky everything has come together in time. The house is ready for occupation. Our electricity is on, the phone is in. We have hot water."

Without conscious thought Kellie reached for his hand. He grasped it tightly and held on as they went downstairs together where he made the introductions.

The middle-aged court-appointed worker was civil enough, but she kept her distance. They sat down together in the living room to answer her general questions. When she asked to see where the baby would sleep, they took her upstairs for the inspection.

After they returned to the living room she looked at them frankly. "From the information given me, I see you've been married under four months."

"That's right," Philippe murmured.

"But you haven't been together the whole time."

Kellie averted her eyes. "No."

"I'm not making any judgments here, Madame Didier. That's for the court to decide. The baby needs an advocate. It's my job to learn all I can about the environment that will be best suited for him."

"Of course," Kellie agreed.

"Do you work?"

"Not now."

"What did you do?"

"I'm a chef."

"Do you plan to work with a baby in the house?"

"No."

"Why not? Many women combine their housewife duties with a career and still manage to raise their off-spring."

"That's true. But I happen to believe the first three years of a child's life are crucial to their development. I don't want someone else raising my baby."

"So in three years you plan to return to work?"

"No. I don't imagine I'll get a job until after my children are raised."

"You're planning to add to your family?"

"Yes."

If Kellie hoped to help Philippe win this case, she was prepared to say anything to give him the ammunition he needed. It was only the truth. Their little addition was already three months along.

"Have you ever had experience being around babies for any length of time?"

"No. I was an only child."

"What makes you think you're qualified to raise one?"

"I don't think anyone is qualified. You learn as you go along."

She felt Philippe's hand at the back of her neck with

a sense of wonder. If he'd put on this display of affection to show the other woman he was attracted to his wife, he'd done it very naturally.

"What about you, Monsieur Didier? Have you been around babies?"

"Yes. I've diapered, fed and tended every one of my nieces and nephews, but as my wife said, it's the doing throughout the years that gives you the experience."

"I expect with your resources you'll be hiring a nanny."

The question caused Kellie's heart to pound so hard, she thought it would jump right out of its cavity. Could he feel it against the hand that was rubbing her back?

"Should we be lucky enough to win custody of Jean-Luc, we plan to invite his grandmother to live with us. There's a private apartment for her."

So Analise was going to be the nanny?

The other woman frowned. "Has she already agreed?"

"No. She doesn't know that's what we have in mind."

"You've never suggested it?"

"My husband wouldn't resort to bribery in the hope of swaying her or the judge," Kellie defended.

"I'm glad to hear it," the social worker murmured. "I think those are all the questions I have. According to my information, your court date is set for next week. Good luck to you. I'll see myself out."

Philippe's hand slid away. He moved quickly to open the front door for her. Kellie followed.

When Madame Frouneau had gone, he shut it. This time when he turned to Kellie, she saw a look of solemnity in his eyes. What was running through his mind now? Was he upset with her?

"I was going to wait until the judge made a decision before showing you the extent of my appreciation for all your help."

Showing me?

"But your unflinching honesty with the social worker has prompted me to do it now. You were very fierce when you sprang to my defense, by the way. For that you deserve a reward. Come out in back with me."

Kellie couldn't imagine what he was talking about.

"You don't have to do anything for me!" she cried as she ran through the house after him.

He'd opened the French doors off the kitchen. When she caught up to him, he said, "There's a reason why I haven't talked to you about the greenhouse."

"I know. The grounds are your department."

"Not any longer."

She blinked. "What do you mean?"

Her husband regarded her for a breathless moment. "You said you wanted to live in Switzerland for the rest of your life. When you give the word, an architect I've hired will transform it into a restaurant where you can cook your French cuisine to your heart's content. It will be a small, exclusive establishment.

"There's plenty of parking, a garden which can be replanted, a charming château to provide the backdrop and create an atmosphere you couldn't duplicate anywhere else."

She'd heard what he'd said, but she still didn't comprehend it.

"This is your home."

He shook his attractive head. "Only if I win custody of Jean-Luc. In that case, I'll ask Analise to live in the house with me. The tower will be yours. You'll be able to run your restaurant without problem."

"Even though we'd be divorced?"

He gave an elegant shrug of his shoulders. "Why not?"

To live next door to your ex-spouse and not care—that meant her husband had to have lost all feeling for her.

She groaned inwardly. Why didn't he just run her through with a sword and be done with it?

"If I lose custody," he went on talking as if he were discussing the weather, "I'll live at the apartment and give you this property in its entirety. In that case you might even want to turn the château into an inn."

What?

"All you'd need to do is put different locks on the bedroom doors. You could transform the garage into an office. The setup is perfect to make this a showplace that will put you on the map."

His guilt over not being able to take her back into his mind and heart was responsible for this extravagant gift which, in reality, was her honorable husband's version of alimony.

Of course she didn't intend to take advantage of such generosity. But for the time being, she would play along and let him think she was thrilled.

When the custody fight was over, she'd inform him of his impending fatherhood and tell him she had no intention of holding him to his fabulous offer.

"I'm overwhelmed, Philippe." She *was* overwhelmed. Only Philippe could have come up with something like this. Her love for him just kept growing deeper.

"You've presented me with a dream beyond my comprehension. I always knew you were a selfless man. If you're sure this is what you really want to do, then

I accept your magnificent present and thank you from the bottom of my heart.''

''Good. I'm glad you're pleased.''

He sounded relieved, as if some great burden he'd been carrying had finally been lifted from his shoulders.

That's what she'd been. A burden.

''What would you think if I moved my things from the apartment to the tower this evening?''

One black brow dipped lower than the other. ''You don't want to stay in the château now that we can sleep here tonight?''

''You know me,'' she flashed him her brightest smile. ''I fell in love with the tower. It's so exciting to think it's going to be mine. I can invite that architect over and we'll start planning out my fantasy restaurant. It will give me something I can sink my teeth into while we wait to go to court. What did you say his name was?''

''It's a woman,'' he muttered in a sober tone. ''Michelle Viret.''

A new love interest for him? Kellie's wounds continued to bleed.

''I'm looking forward to meeting her.'' She rubbed her palms against her jeans, anxious to get away from him before she revealed her anguish. ''Is there anything more you want to do here?'' It was already quarter to six.

''Not that I'm aware of.''

''Then let's go back to the apartment for dinner. I'll fix us an omelette before you get together with your friends. While you're gone, I'll bring another load of my belongings back here.''

''Did I say I was going over to Raoul's?'' he asked in a quiet voice.

Uh-oh.

"No. The other day in the boat when he extended the invitation, I just assumed you'd want to watch your old climbing videos with them."

His eyes were half-veiled. "After I get us settled, I might drop in."

Didn't he know his friends were dying to be with him again?

"Then let's not waste any more time."

For the next two hours she was the one who felt compelled to make conversation. Her taciturn husband could only be described as out-of-sorts. She attributed it to the fact that he'd been pushing himself too long and hard physically to get everything done at the château. Unfortunately they still needed to bring more things from their apartment.

Tomorrow he was going to put in a full day at the office. He probably couldn't wait to be back at the helm.

Once her car was packed, she left the apartment first and made a detour to a lumber yard for a bundle of wood. As soon as she pulled up to the château, she was determined to get a fire going before she did anything else. They'd had the chimneys cleaned. Everything was ready.

She balled up some old newspaper and put the kindling on the top. In minutes shadows from the flames danced against the round wall. There was a nice draw. The heat felt good against the cold outside.

Two trips to the car and she'd brought all her clothes in. She laid them on the bed and pulled the couch up to the hearth, too tired to do any more work tonight.

When Philippe walked in without knocking, she was lying on the cushions warming herself. The lady of the castle.

"Why didn't you wait for me to help you?"

Her handsome knight had gone from out-of-sorts, to angry. She couldn't deal with it. Not tonight.

"Because I don't expect you to wait on me."

His mouth tightened into a thin line before he started hanging her clothes in the closet.

Kellie must have been more exhausted than she thought. Oblivion took over. She didn't remember anything else until she discovered she was lying on top of the sheets of her bed without her shoes or socks.

Disoriented, she murmured, "Philippe?"

The room was dark except for some dying embers in the grate. Through bleary eyes she could barely discern his masculine features. He was close enough for her to feel his breath on her cheek. An explosion of desire shot through her pregnant body.

"Let me help you off with this sweater, then you can go back to sleep." His hands started to tug it over her head.

In an instant she was wide-awake.

"No!" she cried out in absolute panic. Rolling away from him, she clawed at her sweater in an effort to hide the thickening at her waist.

She felt the mattress give. His hand slid up her back to her neck. He massaged the soft skin beneath her hair.

"Kellie—" His voice sounded ragged. He began kneading her shoulder with gentle insistence. "I didn't mean to frighten you. I only wanted to help you get more comfortable."

His touch made her tremble. Hopefully he'd think it was from the cold. "T-thank you, but I'm fine just the way I am. My sweater feels good. You go on to Raoul's. I'll see you in the morning before you leave for the office."

"I've decided I'm too tired to do anything more than stretch out on your couch. Do you mind?"

For him to want to stay in the tower meant he'd probably put too much stress on his knee and it was hurting again. Naturally he couldn't face trying to climb the château stairs. No wonder he'd taken the trouble to carry her to the bed. But now he was paying the price.

"No. Of course not. My grandmother's quilt is on the top shelf of the closet. Use that to put over you."

His hand remained on her shoulder for a breathless moment. She wanted him so badly she was waiting for him to turn her around and crush his mouth against hers. When he drew the covers to her shoulders instead, she had to bury her face in the pillow to stifle her protest.

While she lay there aching for him, her eyelids grew heavy once more. It took a ray of sunshine invading the tower to bring her back to consciousness. With it came a remembrance of the night before.

Philippe!

She sat up in the bed to see if he was still asleep on the couch. All that remained was the white quilt which he'd folded over the end.

Devastated he'd gone, Kellie knew she should be feeling exactly the opposite! Last night had been too close a call. What if he'd discovered the truth?

Under no circumstances did she want to do anything to provoke Philippe's wrath, not when their court date was only six days away. He would tell her to get out as he'd done once before. Then he'd lose the slim chance he had to get custody of Jean-Luc.

The trick was to spend the rest of the week working with the architect he'd hired. At least that way Kellie would know the woman wasn't spending her time with Philippe!

As for her husband, he could go back to earning a living.

By some miracle, photographers and journalists had been banned from Neuchâtel's hall of justice. It wasn't until she and Philippe were riding in the tinted limousine Raoul had provided for them that she learned he'd used his influence with the judge to keep the closed door proceedings private.

The debt she and her husband owed the Mertiers continued to grow.

Honore met them at the entrance and escorted them inside the near-empty courtroom.

Analise nodded to them from her seat in the audience. Jean-Luc wasn't with her. She must have found a neighbor to baby-sit.

They sat down at the table with Honore who always looked very distinguished and professional. Across the aisle from them sat Jean-Luc's birthfather.

He was dark, reasonably nice looking. Probably not six feet. Kellie noticed right away he had a stocky build. The baby bore a strong resemblance to him.

His whole attention seemed to be focused on Philippe even though his attorney was talking to him.

Philippe had never looked more dashing to Kellie. Formally dressed in a midnight blue, hand-tailored suit, she couldn't keep her eyes off him.

Other than a bailiff standing near a set of double doors, that represented the full complement of people assembled.

Honore leaned over to kiss her on both cheeks. "Did I tell you how stunning you look?"

She'd chosen to wear a new two-piece black wool

suit that hid her fuller figure. Deciding to wear her hair back, she tied it at the nape with a black print scarf.

Philippe heard the aside and turned his head toward her. His dark eyes seemed to take in every detail of her face and figure. "Black's always been your best color."

Heat filled her cheeks. "Thank you. Both of you."

"Nervous?" Honore smiled.

"Do you have to ask?"

"Just follow my lead."

For some reason Philippe seemed to be the calm one today. He actually sat there in a relaxed position as if he knew something the rest of them didn't know. As if he were a mere spectator.

The bailiff told them to rise.

Kellie watched as the sixtyish-looking judge entered through the double doors. He took his seat before them, put on his glasses and acknowledged the two solicitors present. The proceedings were being held in French. Every canton had their own individual court procedure. This one seemed quite informal.

The judge reviewed the facts of the case aloud and then called on Honore to present his client for questioning.

Kellie clasped her hands beneath the table to hide their trembling. She said a little prayer as she followed Philippe's progress to the witness chair. Once he was sworn in, Honore approached him.

"Monsieur Didier—the court has reviewed all the particulars in this case. It has been proved conclusively that you are not the birthfather of Jean-Luc, yet you are petitioning for custody. Will you explain before this bench why you're pursuing such an action?"

Philippe sat forward. "When Yvette came to my office to tell me she was having my baby, she was eight months pregnant. The time frame coincided with my trip to Chamonix where I had spent part of a night with her. No matter how unlikely, I accepted the fact that I could have been the father.

"From the time of our car accident on, she had me fairly well convinced I was responsible for her pregnancy. Because she was so ill, I didn't pursue the DNA testing at the time. For one thing, I was still recovering from a knee operation, and she needed comforting.

"I didn't realize until Jean-Luc was born two weeks later that I had bonded with the child in my mind and heart. The last time I ever spoke to Yvette, she begged me to love him. Perhaps she had a presentiment that she was going to die."

The way Philippe's voice shook just then caused Kellie's throat to close up.

"I never did hold the baby or see him up close until several weeks later when his grandmother allowed my wife and I a night's visitation. I think I knew when I looked at him that he couldn't be my son, but it didn't matter. I loved him and felt the longing to be a father to him.

"When the DNA test didn't result in a match, that didn't matter to me either. As my wife said, he's an innocent child who only wants love. That's why we're here today, hoping to become his parents."

"Thank you, *monsieur*. That's all for now."

Kellie lowered her head, fighting for control over her emotions. As Philippe sat down at their table, Jean-Luc's father was sworn in, but she was too distracted to pay much attention.

The need to touch her husband was so powerful, she reached for his hand. He gripped it for a long moment before letting it go.

The opposing counsel got to his feet. "Dr. Bruchard? The court has read your statement that you were in love with Yvette Boiteux. Tell us about that relationship."

"Yvette was already working at the veterinary clinic when I bought into the corporation. We began spending more and more time together at my apartment after hours. I fell in love with her. At one point I told her I wanted to get married and start a family. I didn't have a lot of money, but I could support her if she didn't want to work.

"She said she'd give me her answer after she got home from her ski trip to Chamonix. I begged her not to take her vacation at that time because I hadn't been working at the clinic long enough to take time off to go with her. I promised her a ski honeymoon if she'd wait.

"But she said she'd had it planned before I'd ever joined the clinic. Skiing was her passion. Before she left, she told me she loved me. She asked me to be patient with her.

"What else could I do but say yes? I loved her. But when she came back from her trip, she'd returned a changed person. She told me she'd met a man who'd transformed her life."

Kellie could relate to Yvette's feelings. *Oh, how she could relate.*

"She said that if she couldn't marry him, she wouldn't marry anyone."

By this time the heartbroken vet was so choked up, he couldn't talk. The man wasn't acting. Kellie felt his pain. He'd truly loved Yvette. The judge, everyone in the room knew it.

She bowed her head. His testimony had to be so hard

on Philippe. Again she reached for his hand. This time he held on and didn't let go.

"Yvette cut me off so completely I was shattered. I never saw her again. Months later an acquaintance told me she'd died. I never even had the opportunity to go to her funeral.

"When Yvette's mother called me and told me about the baby, I went to her apartment at once. One look at Jean-Luc and I knew he was our son, my flesh and blood. I want to raise my own boy, your honor."

As the man broke down sobbing, Philippe's hand almost cut off the circulation in hers. When he finally released it, he pulled a pen out of his pocket and wrote something on a piece of paper.

Reaching behind her back, he handed it to Honore. After the other man read it, he stared at Philippe for a moment, then gave him an almost imperceptible smile.

After the vet had been told he could leave the witness seat, Honore asked the judge if his client could say a few more words. The judge nodded and told Philippe to stand where he was.

"Your Honor? Much as I wanted custody of Jean-Luc, after hearing from Dr. Bruchard, it's obvious the baby belongs with his rightful father."

Kellie knew that's what her husband would say, because he was that kind of man. The vet's head jerked toward Philippe in total shock.

"I'm now going to say something that wasn't in any of the written or oral testimonies. I hope it will ease Dr. Bruchard's mind to some degree.

"While a friend and I were climbing in Chamonix, there was an avalanche. We helped the skiers who were caught in it. One of them was Yvette."

A gasp filled the court room. It came from Analise.

Kellie looked over at her, realizing Yvette had never told her mother about her close call with death.

Philippe went on talking. "I flew in the helicopter to the hospital with her. She was fortunate that nothing serious had happened to her, but she was very shaken. After such a traumatic experience for her, she was afraid to be left alone, so I accompanied her back to her hotel and brought her dinner.

"I'm telling the court all this to explain the unique circumstances of that twenty-four-hour period. There's an old saying about loving the person who saves your life. Yvette didn't love me, but she was grateful to me that her life had been spared. I didn't love her. She was a stranger to me. But I was grateful fate had placed me in a position to be able to save her.

"It's a tragedy that illness that took her life so early. But she left a wonderful legacy behind. Jean-Luc. He belongs with the man who loved Yvette and wanted to make a home for them. Therefore, I don't feel it appropriate to waste any more of the court's time. After consulting with my attorney, I withdraw the custody petition."

Oh, Philippe. You wonderful man. I know your heart is heavy, but as soon as we leave this courtroom, I'm going to tell you something that will change your world forever.

The judge summoned the attorneys to the bench. They chatted quietly, then took their seats once more. He looked down at Philippe with an admiring expression.

"The court would like to thank Monsieur Didier for a decision that could not have been made lightly. I have no doubt that little boy would have found a fine home with you and your wife."

His glance switched to the vet. "Dr. Bruchard, you heard Monsieur Didier's declaration. Therefore the court grants you full custody of your son, Jean-Luc Bruchard. Congratulations.

"Court dismissed."

In the next instant Analise hurried down to the their table and threw her arms around Philippe. Her face was awash in tears. "I didn't know you had rescued my darling girl. I didn't know. Forgive me for being so cruel to you."

Philippe stood up and put his arm around her. "There's nothing to forgive."

"Can we still be friends?" Analise's pleading gaze took in Philippe and Kellie.

"Of course." Kellie reached out to hug the older woman. "Thank you for letting my husband have some time with Jean-Luc," she whispered. "It pulled him out of one of the lowest points of his life. For that I will always be grateful."

In the periphery Kellie saw Philippe walk over to Dr. Bruchard and shake his hand. His noble character filled her with awe all over again.

"Surely he won't divorce you now," Analise said in a quiet voice. "Not after everything you've been through."

"I—I'm afraid so."

"But it doesn't make any sense. Your husband's in love with you."

"Once upon a time he was, Analise."

"Nonsense. I spent an evening at your apartment. I know what I saw. He couldn't take his eyes off you."

"That's because he'd suspected I'd done something to get you there. You and I both know he had every reason to be suspicious."

''I didn't hear him complaining,'' the older woman said dryly.

''No. He loves that child. So do I.''

''Then go home with him and do something about it. There are ways around a man, if you get my meaning.'' Her eyes twinkled.

Kellie took a fortifying breath. She loved Yvette's mother. ''I'm going to.'' Just not exactly in the way you mean. ''Thank you for the advice. I'll call you one day soon.''

She felt a hand on her arm. It was Honore. ''Come on. While your husband is still talking to Dr. Bruchard, I'll walk with you down to the limousine.''

Needing no urging, she left the courtroom with him. ''Thank you for helping Philippe,'' she said in a tear-filled voice. ''I know how much he appreciates all you did for him.''

''I did it for both of you.''

''You know what I mean.''

''But I don't think you know what *I* mean.''

Kellie darted him a surprised glance. ''I don't understand.''

They'd reached the underground parking. To her surprise Philippe's car was waiting for them. A parking attendant opened the front passenger door so she could climb in.

''Kellie—'' Honore's eyes peered into her soul. ''There never was any possibility of Philippe winning that custody suit. Not with all his money. Not even with you doing everything you could in the capacity of a loving wife.''

It took a moment for the words to sink in. ''So what are you saying?''

''You're an intelligent woman. I'm going to leave

you alone to figure that out. I have every faith in you, *ma chère*."

He leaned down to kiss her cheek before climbing into the limousine behind Philippe's car. While she was still reeling from the revelation, she caught sight of her husband's tall, male physique as he walked swiftly toward the car.

It was almost time…

CHAPTER NINE

THOUGH Philippe appeared to be as relaxed as he'd been in the courtroom, he hadn't said a word since they'd left the hall of justice.

After handing Jean-Luc over to Dr. Bruchard without a struggle, Kellie knew her husband's heart was breaking. But he wasn't about to let her see his anguish. To her chagrin she couldn't begin to read what was going on behind his inscrutable expression.

All she knew was that he wasn't taking her straight home so she could tell him the news that would make him a new man. Instead he drove to the gates leading to the Château D'Arillac. The guard allowed them to pass through.

Maybe Lee and Raoul had told Philippe to come for lunch once their court case was over. It was very kind of them, but this was one time when she needed to be strictly alone with her husband.

She'd been to the their château several times with Lee since Philippe had bought the house, but she'd never had the time yet to explore the extensive grounds of the royal estate. Through the princess she'd learned that among other things, they had their own riding stable.

Horses were one of the Mertiers passions. Apparently she and Raoul rode most mornings in the surrounding forest which all went to make up their private property.

Both of them had known a lot of pain before they

met. Now they led a fairy-tale life, but that was because they were madly in love. The royal trappings only provided a backdrop.

Kellie might not have been a princess, but for the one month of her marriage to Philippe, she'd led that same fairy-tale life as his wife.

Turning her head away from him, she wondered if she would ever stop grieving over an act on her part that had destroyed something so rare and precious.

To her surprise he didn't turn into the driveway that led to Raoul's private entrance. Instead they continued along the tree-lined driveway past the château which led to the woods covering the lower hillside. Another minute and they came to a building hidden among the trees. Philippe pulled to a stop.

She looked over at him in confusion. "What is this place?"

"The royal kennel."

Kennel?

"Since you're going to be living alone on the property, you need a good guard dog. Raoul's favorite black lab had a litter of pups some time ago. They're old enough now to leave their mother. There's one I've had my eye on, but you're free to choose the pup that catches your eye."

Kill her with kindness. That's what Philippe was doing, but enough was enough.

He started to get out of the car to help her, but she grabbed hold of his arm.

"No, Philippe!"

He stared back at her in puzzlement. "You grew up loving your grandfather's labrador before it died."

"That's true. But I c-couldn't handle another dog right now."

"Raoul has a man who will help train it for you if that's your worry."

"It isn't!" she cried.

Lines formed, darkening his features. "What's wrong, Kellie? What's going on?"

"Please could we go back to the house first? Then I'll tell you."

He had to know the truth *now,* but she refused to make her confession on someone else's property, even his best friend's. Philippe deserved to be in his own home when she told him something that would change both their lives forever.

He backed his car around so fast, she gripped the armrests for support. Gone was the man at the courthouse who'd been relaxed and in control. The way he was negotiating the twists and turns back to the gate of the estate, they might as well have been racing in the Grand Prix at Monte Carlo.

Once allowed past the guard, they sped the short distance home. As soon as he pulled to a shrieking stop in the parking area, she got out of the car.

"If you don't mind, I'd like to change out of this suit, then I'll join you in the living room of the house."

She shut the door and starting running across the lawn, heedless of her pregnant condition. Within seconds he'd caught up to her. Grasping her arm, he guided her into the house.

After slamming the front door behind them, he let her go. His eyes glittered with anger. It was the look she'd seen at the chalet when he'd discovered her lurking in the kitchen.

"All right. We're home. What is going on? I want an answer, Kellie."

"Could we sit down?"

"No."

He stood there like a dark colossus waiting for an explanation. The time had come.

"Philippe?" she began in a tremulous voice.

He didn't say anything, but she could tell he was listening because the moment she spoke his name, a grimace marred his features.

Her mouth went dry, making it impossible to moisten her lips. "D-do you remember that night at the hospital when you said there was something you had to tell me?"

A weightier silence greeted her question.

Of course he remembered! What a ghastly, insensitive way to begin what had to be said.

"After I flew home to Washington, I started getting headaches and ended up going to our family doctor for a checkup. T-that's when I found out tha—"

This was so much harder than she'd imagined it would be.

"Found out *what?*" he demanded with stunning ferocity.

"We're going to have a baby."

Instant stillness permeated the foyer.

She kneaded her hands.

"I know this comes as a tremendous shock to you. It did to me, too, but it shouldn't have. Not when we'd talked about starting a family right away."

Kellie finally dared to look at him. He stared at her as if he were transfixed.

"The doctor referred me to an obstetrician named Dr. Cutler. At that point in time I was six weeks along. He estimates the delivery date for our baby is June 14."

While she waited for Philippe to say something, her whole life seemed to flash before her eyes.

"Did you find out before or after you knew Yvette had died in childbirth?"

There it was. The question she'd been dreading. The one question whose answer would lead him to believe it was the only reason she came back to Switzerland. It was the only question that mattered to Philippe.

"Before."

She heard his sharp intake of breath.

"Darling—" she cried out in panic. "I only learned of my condition just before I found out about Yvette's tragic death!

"If there hadn't been extenuating circumstances, you *must* know I would have told you immediately. But after your accident and everything you were struggling with, I was afraid to make things any more complicated for you."

He let out an epithet that raised the hairs on the back of her neck. "So—you decided to play God with my life a second time."

Her honesty had come three months too late.

"What kind of a wife shoves her husband at another woman for the sake of a child who might or might not be his, yet would keep all knowledge of the baby they'd made together a *secret?*"

"I'm sorry, darling. You'll never know how sorry." Her face glistened with tears. "I realize now I should have phoned you with the news the second I got home from the doctor. But I was a fool back then. I did everything wrong.

"When I came to my senses, you had already fallen in love with Jean-Luc. I felt it was more important to help you win custody of him first."

"*Mon Dieu.* First you use Raoul, then Honore," he lashed out. "When I warned you at the chalet it was too late for any elaborate ploys to fix what was wrong between us, it never occurred to me your trump card would be our baby.''

Long ago from a hospital bed, Philippe had risked ruining their marriage with his confession. The risk hadn't paid off. She'd done the worst thing a wife could do. Instead of standing by him, she'd left him and filed for a divorce.

Now their positions were reversed. She'd just taken an enormous risk with *her* confession. At this late date she'd given him every reason to despise her forever.

Defeated beyond hope she said, ''It wasn't a scheme to get closer to you. I knew you'd think that. But you'd be wrong. I've been waiting this long to tell you the truth so you could focus on Jean-Luc. In case the court didn't rule in your favor, it's been my dream to give you a gift no one could ever take from you.''

Raw pain filled his eyes which were suspiciously bright, even for Philippe at his most vulnerable. ''I really *don't* know you, do I?'' he whispered in such a bleak voice she wanted to die.

In the next instant he whipped past her and disappeared out the door. Within seconds she heard the squeal of tires as he drove off. At the speed he was going, it wouldn't surprise her to hear later he'd been in another accident.

Please, God. Don't let that happen. Their baby needed its father.

Oh where to turn? Right now she needed a friend. Someone to talk to who knew Philippe better than anyone else besides Raoul.

She dashed to the study and phoned the Didiers' home in Paris. ''Claudine?'' she cried when heard her friend's voice.

"Kellie— I was praying you'd call! Honore has already told us the bad news. My brother's too damn noble for his own good," her voice throbbed. "How is he?"

"T-that's what I wanted to talk to you about. Oh Claudine— I don't know what to do."

"Where are you?"

"At our new house."

"Where's Philippe?"

Her eyes closed tightly. "He's gone."

There was a period of quiet.

"You mean as in *really* gone?"

"I don't know!" Kellie wailed in agony.

"Something else has to be wrong then. What haven't you told me? No, don't answer that. As soon as I hang up, I'm flying there on the company jet. I should be with you in an hour. Don't you dare do anything crazy like leave before I get there."

The receiver was soaking wet. "I—I won't. Do you know the address?"

"*Bien sur.* I should think everyone in French Switzerland knows the location of the Château des Fleurs. I'd be insanely jealous if it were anyone but you living there."

"Castle of flowers?" Kellie murmured.

"Yes. It was built as compensation for the second son of an Arillac whose elder brother was crowned prince. His only pleasure came from cultivating flowers. In its original state, the gardens were so fabulous, I understand people came from every canton to see them.

"Until now only royalty has been allowed to live there. For Prince Raoul to allow it to be sold to Philippe tells you of his deep affection for your husband. I'll tell you more when I get there. *À bientôt, chère amie.*"

Stunned by the revelation on top of her grief, Kellie hung up the phone and went directly to the tower. After she'd changed into jeans and a loose fitting blouse, she threw on a jacket and walked out to the pier to wait for Claudine.

As soon as her friend arrived, they could go for a boat ride. In anticipation, Kellie unsnapped the cover and found the key to the ignition in the side pocket where Philippe always kept it hidden.

Battle weary in heart and soul, she made a bed out of the padded seats and lay down on her back to look at the overcast sky.

A breeze had come up on the lake, lowering the air temperature. She welcomed its bite. The rocking of the boat against the pier was very soothing. The next thing she knew she could hear Claudine's voice calling to her.

Kellie sat up too fast and got a cramp in her side. "Over here, Claudine!" She scrambled to the driver's seat and blew the horn.

"I wondered where you were!" Her brunette friend ran on to the pier and jumped into the boat.

"Thank you for coming," Kellie half-sobbed the words.

They hugged for a long moment before Claudine eased away from her first. Her dark brown eyes were so much like Philippe's it was uncanny. They dropped to Kellie's stomach.

When they lifted again she cried, "*Mon Dieu*—how far along are you?"

There could be no secrets from Claudine.

"Thirteen weeks."

Her expressive face turned serious. "When did my brother find out?"

"Today. After court."

Claudine groaned.

"A-as soon as I told him, he accused me of playing God with his life a second time and left with his tires digging up the gravel. I'm surprised you didn't see the ruts!"

"Oh, Kellie—"

Then she hugged her again. "How absolutely fantastic! I'm so happy for both of you I could dance across the lake." She patted Kellie's little tummy. "I'm going to have a niece or nephew who'll be half American. When the family hears this news, it will pull them out of a pit they've been in since the accident."

Kellie shuddered. Claudine put an affectionate hand on her arm. "Don't look so tragic. It is not the end of the world. This is the beginning."

Tears blurred Kellie's eyes. "How I wish I believed that. Philippe loathes the very sight of me."

"Really." Her lovely Gallic features mocked Kellie. "So explain the reason why he bought the Château des Fleurs."

"He did it for Jean-Luc."

"Ah yes? He bought a small palace from a prince for a little child? I think you and I need a heart-to-heart."

"I'd like that, but not here. Let's go for a ride in the boat where we can be alone." She pulled two life jackets from the locker and handed one of them to Claudine.

"You mean before he decides to come back?" They both put them on and cinched the straps.

"Something like that, yes."

"You're really afraid of him, aren't you."

"No...yes...but not in the way you mean."

Claudine's eyes narrowed. "Come on. I'll undo the ropes."

Kellie started the motor. After Claudine jumped in,

Kellie began to reverse away from the pier. For a few minutes they traveled at a steady speed, then she pushed on the throttle and they headed for open water.

Her glance took in the sky. It looked a little darker than it was before her brief nap, but there were other boats including a couple of sailboats still taking runs.

Deciding to remain on the side of caution, she only drove their boat another mile, then cut the engine so they could slowly drift back toward the pier with the help of the wind.

''We are alone now, my friend. I want to hear every detail from the moment Princess Lee arrived in the Ville d'Eaton.'' It was one of the many little jokes she'd made that had endeared her to Kellie's grandfather.

It was so easy to talk to Claudine. For the next half hour, all the pain and the anguish that had been locked up for so long came spilling out.

''The thing is, Claudine, I'll do anything Philippe wants so he can be near his child. He'll have daily access if that's his wish. We'll work out the visitation to make him happy. But I can't stay at the château.

''It's not just because of its royal history. You have to see I've done nothing to deserve such a grand scale of generosity. Naturally I understand he wants to be responsible for the baby. Of course he wants me to live in a decent place. So do I. But not at the estate. Raoul intended for Philippe to live there. Not his divorced wife!

''You're close to Philippe. How do I tell him without making the wall higher between us?''

She gave a Gallic shrug of her shoulders. ''You don't.''

''Claudine—''

Her dark eyes flashed. ''Aren't you the one who asked for my opinion?''

''Yes.''

''Then take it and stay where you are! Philippe is right about you in one sense. You *do* try to orchestrate everything. It's always with the best of intentions, of course. You want everyone to be happy. But life can't always be structured like that, as you've found out to your detriment.''

Claudine was only speaking the truth.

''For once, why don't you stop thinking. Just take one day at a time. You need to concentrate on yourself and the baby.

''If he didn't adore you, he wouldn't have bought the Château des Fleurs or given you carte blanche to decorate it the way you wanted. As for the greenhouse being turned into a restaurant, you can be certain Philippe obtained Raoul's approval long before now.

''Once and for all, give my brother a chance to orchestrate things for a change. He may surprise you.''

Kellie had been listening.

She finally lifted her head to tell Claudine she would take her advice when a big wave slapped hard against the boat, soaking them in spray.

Distracted for the moment, she looked out over the water. While they'd been talking, whitecaps had formed. The shore appeared farther away than ever. They'd been pushed across the lake and were halfway to the other side which was still about two and a half miles away. By now the sky was filled with thunderheads.

''We've got to go back right now.''

Claudine nodded, white-faced.

Without wasting any time, Kellie started the motor and turned the boat in the direction of their pier.

The wind had grown fierce. She'd never seen a storm like this on the lake before. There was no way she could speed through the swells. The twenty-eight-mile-long body of water resembled an ocean.

"Oh *Mon Dieu—*" Claudine cried out in terror. "Look over there!"

Kellie was concentrating hard on keeping the boat from capsizing. As she lifted her eyes in the direction Claudine was pointing, her heart almost failed her.

A funnel had formed from one of the blackest clouds. She watched in horror as it touched down on the lake and started coming in their direction.

"That's a waterspout!"

Once when she'd been out boating with Philippe, he told her the lake's proximity to the Jura mountains produced waterspouts, mostly during the summer months. But sometimes they happened during storms as late as October and November. This was one of those rare times.

He'd warned her that if she ever sighted one while out on the water, she should make a ninety-degree turn away from the direction it was coming and head like hell for shore.

Following his advice, she turned the wheel, but she had to keep the speed down to negotiate the waves.

Claudine was too terrified to scream. She kept crossing herself. That was good. They needed all the help they could get to survive this.

Kellie never looked back. She didn't dare or she'd probably pass out with fright. To make things worse, it began raining. Not in drops, but sheets!

If the downpour continued for any length of time, the

boat would be swamped. Kellie found herself muttering a prayer as they plowed through the angry water. Visibility was now zero.

"We're g-going to d-die, Kellie." Between fright and the freezing cold elements, both their teeth were chattering.

"N-no we're n-not! We're g-going to live!"

I have a child to raise with Philippe.

It seemed like they'd been going nowhere for hours when suddenly they crashed against some wood pilings. Claudine was knocked to the floor of the boat. The impact pressed Kellie hard against the steering wheel. Thanks to her life preserver which acted like an air bag, she felt no pain.

Almost immediately she heard some people shouting. Before she knew it, strangers had helped pull her and Claudine out of the boat. From what she could gather, it was a middle-aged couple. They owned a vineyard near the shore and introduced themselves as Valerie and Louis Charriere.

"Are you all right?"

"Can you walk?"

She and Claudine both answered yes.

"Come in the house," the woman urged. "You must get warm and dry."

The hospitality for which Switzerland was famous had never been in more evidence.

At Kellie's request, Louis said he would contact Philippe. His wife hustled them inside their house. She handed them robes. It was heaven to be able to take a shower and enjoy hot soup afterward.

Valerie was like a fairy godmother. Their clothes had already been washed and were now drying. While they tucked into a second bowl of what Kellie considered a hearty beef stew, Louis entered the kitchen with their purses. He smiled at Kellie.

"I just spoke to your frantic husband. He'll be here shortly."

Claudine's gaze darted to Kellie's with that I-told-you-so look in her eyes. The thought of seeing Philippe sent a thrill through her body.

"We heard the severe weather warning and went out to secure our boat. That's when we saw yours headed toward our pier."

"I'm sorry our boat ran into it. You couldn't see anything out there for a little while. We'll pay you for the damage."

"Let's not worry about that now."

After the soup, she made them hot chocolate. "Drink it! After such a scare, you need the sugar."

Valerie waited on them with the same care she would have given one of her own children. Soon their clothes were dry, even their sneakers. A few minutes later she and Claudine were fully dressed again and felt renewed.

They went back to the kitchen to thank Valerie for everything. While they stood talking, Louis walked in the kitchen followed by two tall, strikingly handsome men, one of whom was still dressed in midnight-blue trousers. She hardly recognized the damp, dirt-stained shirt as the one he'd worn to court. The tie was gone along with his suit jacket.

Valerie cried out, "Prince Raoul!"

But Kellie's eyes were focused on Philippe who no longer looked like the angry man who had driven off hours earlier with no hint that he would ever be back.

His pronounced pallor bespoke the true state of his emotions as he came closer to reach for her and

Claudine at the same time. His strong arms went around both of them.

"Thank God you're safe!" His voice trembled with a huskiness that bespoke his suffering. He hugged them tighter. Kellie felt him bury his face in her hair and kiss her as if she were something precious.

"Raoul and I were at his château when he was informed of the storm warning. We hurried down to the pier to secure his boat, then drove over to secure ours. That's the moment we saw the waterspout."

Kellie could feel the sinews in his arms harden as if he were reliving his terror.

"*Mon Dieu*—when I discovered the boat was missing and you two weren't anywhere around—"

"Thanks to Kellie's quick thinking and courage, we are alive and well," Claudine broke in. "I'm ashamed to say that if it had been up to me, we would still be out there somewhere."

"That's not true," Kellie defended her friend.

"Oh, yes, it is. You knew exactly what you were doing while I just sat there waiting for the inevitable to happen. I'm very ashamed of myself."

"All I did was remember what Philippe told me to do if I ever saw one of those coming."

Kellie eased away from her husband's arm enough to look up at him. "I'll always be thankful for those words of wisdom. They saved the three of us."

She watched him swallow hard before his gaze dropped to her stomach covered by the blouse.

He gathered her against him once more. "Let's go home." He whispered the words against her ear where she felt the brush of his lips. His touch traveled through her body like a current of electricity.

Over his broad shoulder she saw Claudine's eyes

gleam with an unspoken message. It said, "Don't think, my friend. Just go with the moment and see what happens."

That's exactly what Kellie intended to do.

The next few minutes passed in a blur as they thanked the Charrieres for everything they'd done. Kellie heard her husband promise they would be repaid for their help. Then Raoul assisted Claudine out to his Land Rover.

While they got in the front, Philippe helped Kellie into the back. When he was seated and had shut the door, he pulled her onto his lap. She melted against him, unable to believe she was finally where she'd always wanted to be.

He crushed her in his arms without saying anything, but she could hear the strong pounding of his heart against hers. They were communing in the age-old way.

Words would come later. Right now all that mattered was to be held in his embrace. She would do as Claudine advised and just *feel* instead of think.

In the front seat Raoul had asked Claudine for a blow by blow account of what had happened on the lake. It was cathartic for her to work the tension out of her system by telling him about their harrowing experience. He made an exceptional listener.

Kellie loved Raoul for being such an incredible friend to all of them, but especially to her husband.

It seemed that when Philippe had left her in the foyer, he'd driven to Raoul's instead of speeding out on the highway where he might have been injured. No matter what an expert he was behind the wheel of a car, he wouldn't have been paying attention, not when certain demons were driving him.

His solid masculine warmth, the familiar smell of his

skin combined with the scent of the soap he always used in the shower—all mingled to arouse desires she'd had to suppress these last few months.

It was automatic to burrow her face in his neck. She found herself kissing him. She couldn't help it.

When his breath caught, she realized he was barely holding on to his control. Kellie had made love with her husband too many times not to pick up on the signals that meant he could hardly wait to get her alone.

She lifted her head to gently bite his earlobe. For some reason that had always been one of his sensitive spots. She enjoyed driving him crazy there.

He was going crazy now. She could feel it in his body tension.

The second Raoul pulled the Land Rover to a stop in their parking area, Philippe jumped out of the back seat so fast with her, she didn't have time to blink.

The storm had passed over. Everything was dripping wet, but at least the rain had stopped.

Raoul leaned out his window. "Claudine's going to spend tonight with Lee and me. See you two around."

He backed up in a hurry and drove away.

CHAPTER TEN

BEFORE Kellie could countenance it, Philippe had picked her up in hard-muscled arms. He started across the lawn with her.

She thought he would take her inside the château. Instead he headed for the tower. He moved with effortless male grace. From watching videos, she knew her husband climbed mountains the same way, making it look easy.

Kellie didn't know how he could see where he was going with her long hair spilling all over his face and arm. But he seemed oblivious as his strides brought them closer to their destination.

When he pushed the door open without having to use a key, she realized he must have come in here earlier looking for her and hadn't bothered to lock it.

Again he surprised her by removing her jacket and lowering her to the couch rather than the bed. But Kellie had learned her lessons the hard way and didn't question his actions.

He pulled off her shoes and stockings as he'd done last week, then found the white quilt and put it over her. Their eyes met and clung in feverish anticipation of what was about to come.

"I'm going to build a fire," he murmured, bending over to brush his lips against hers. "Don't move."

"I wouldn't dream of it," she responded in a trembling voice.

Loving every centimeter of his powerful body, she

watched him hunker down. Out of need, she caressed his back while he worked. Within minutes the kindling had caught fire. He put two logs on top of it, then turned to her.

Kissing the palm that had been touching him he said, "I need a shower."

"Hurry," she begged him.

His eyes glowed with desire. He reached out and slid his hand over her jeans to the hard little mound where their unborn baby lived. She saw unabashed joy spread over his face.

Too soon he got to his feet and disappeared into the bathroom.

It had grown dark out. A steady wind blew, filling the tower with its mournful sounds. Firelight flickered against the walls. There could be no place in the world more romantic.

Back again with her beloved husband, she could honestly say she'd never been this happy in her entire life. In a few minutes she would show him what he meant to her.

Her heart raced when he came in by the fire with a towel riding low around his hips. His dark male beauty took her breath.

He pulled back the quilt and knelt at the side of the couch to look at her. His gaze took in the changes to her body. Her eyes closed when she felt his mouth kiss her belly. Then it fell on hers. They both moaned in ecstasy as he carried her to the bed.

They made love on and off throughout the night. Each time was like the first. Their passion for each other was too overwhelming for talk. There were so many things waiting to be said, but this night was a time out of time. Their sensual needs had overpowered them. The words would come later.

Kellie opened her eyes when a spoke of sunlight made its appearance across the bed, warming her hand that lay on top of the covers. Her husband's right leg held her left one trapped.

It felt so good to wake up that way, she turned her head toward him, longing to know his possession once more.

"Philippe?"

"Mmm?"

"Are you awake?"

"Do you want me to be?" His deep voice told her he was still asleep.

Disappointed, she bit her lip. "I want what you want."

He chuckled and pulled her into his arms. "My insatiable wife. Pregnancy has made you more exciting than ever."

She kissed his compelling mouth. "I hope you're still saying that when I'm ready to deliver."

He opened his eyes. This morning they were more brown than black between his dark lashes. His expression grew serious.

"When you left for Washington, I found out how much I truly loved you. The pain of loss was so acute, it turned me into someone I'm ashamed of. I never want to experience that agony again. It's a miracle you came back to me, let alone that I have any friends left."

She shuddered. "It was all my fault for hurting you, darling. Forgive me."

He heaved a tortured sigh. "I'm the one who needs to ask your forgiveness. Kellie—I'm anything but the noble, honorable man you seem to think I am."

"Oh, yes, you are. I was in court with you yesterday, remember? What you did for Jean-Luc's father won everyone's admiration."

"That's what I'm talking about, *mon amour.* I've lied and manipulated so many situations, it's time I confessed."

He was serious.

"About what?"

"For openers, I never had any intention of telling you about Yvette."

Surprised, Kellie sat all the way up in the bed. He propped himself on his side with the pillow and eyed her somberly.

"Until she showed up at my office, I'd honestly believed that what had happened between us in Chamonix was the result of her close call with death. But the fact that she waited until her eighth month to come forward made me realize she had a mercenary side to her nature which I hadn't suspected.

"When we reached her apartment, my plan was to tell her that I would get in touch with my attorney who would order DNA tests done once the baby was born. In my gut I was ninety-nine percent sure it would prove Jean-Luc wasn't mine.

"If it turned out I was the father, then I would be financially responsible for it and try to be the best father I could. At that point I would tell my wife the truth. But until the tests were done, she was to say nothing that could ever get back to you.

"I was so shaken to think she was in my life for any reason, let alone that she'd shown up on the night of our first month anniversary, I never saw that other car coming. The accident changed all my best-laid plans."

"That was such a horrible night," she whispered.

"When you came in the cubicle, you looked like a vision. I had a struggle with my conscience. Should I take my chances on your not finding out, knowing Yvette was in the same E.R. room with us?

"Or, should I bare my soul to you and pray you loved me enough to take as much of the truth as I thought you could handle?

"What would be worse? A lie I could be caught in before the night was over, one you might never forgive? Or the pain I would cause you when you heard the truth?

"I chose the latter, holding on to the belief that once you'd endured your initial anguish, you'd still be able to find it in your heart to love me."

She shook her head. "I could never stop loving you. It wouldn't be possible. My letter explained the issues that drove me away."

He grasped her hand, almost crushing it between both of his. "Do you know that before she came to the office, I could hardly contain my excitement because I had a special gift for you."

Her eyes searched his. "What?"

"The royal deed to our home. Raoul gave me the Château des Fleurs for the small part I played so he could get out of his betrothal to Princess Sophie and marry Lee. He put it my hands before I followed you back to Washington."

"I don't believe it!"

"When I told him I couldn't accept his gift, he told me he would never forgive me if I didn't. He said he'd always wanted a brother, and if he could have chosen one, it would have been me."

"Everyone loves you, darling."

He caressed her cheek. "Raoul went on to say that

if it would make me feel better, I could donate something to one of the charities he sponsored.''

Kellie's mind was reeling. ''So that means all those houses we looked at with Monsieur Penot—''

''It was pure bluff. I paid him a handsome tip to pretend in front of you.''

''Philippe!''

''There's more, but first I have to apologize for accusing you of using Raoul. He knew when he came to my apartment that I was on the verge of some kind of breakdown.

''After I'd recovered from my operation enough to return to the apartment, Marcel helped me inside. I saw the table you'd prepared for our special dinner. I hobbled over to it with my crutches and read the message you'd left on my plate.

''By the time I'd opened the box and examined the cuff links you'd made me with the flowers I'd given you, I was in agony because I knew how much the truth would have hurt you.

''But it was when I read your goodbye letter that I lost it, Kellie. I really lost it. Marcel called my doctor. He came over and gave me a sedative.

''After everyone left, I went to bed. When I got up, I didn't particularly care whether I lived or died. Marcel phoned my brother to come and fill in until I was fit for work. I refused to see anyone. But Raoul had a way of breaking me down until I finally let him in. You know the rest.''

Kellie wrapped her arms around him. They rocked back and forth.

''It wasn't until yesterday when I ended up on his doorstep that he set me straight about sending Lee to bring you home to me.''

"I'm so thankful she came!" Kellie blurted. "Poor Claudine had tried to stop me from sending those divorce papers, but I was so full of my self-righteous ideas of what you should or shouldn't do, I wouldn't listen to what your sister was trying to tell me.

"It took hearing Lee's voice, looking into her eyes, to make me realize what a horrible thing I'd done to you. I couldn't get back to you fast enough. When Raoul picked us up in Geneva, he let me know in his own kind way that I'd really hurt you. I'm indebted to them both.

"But the truth is, if I hadn't heard anything before too much longer, I would have phoned Claudine to find out information. The result would have been the same. I would have flown back to Switzerland, but I would have found a different way to approach you."

"*Mon Dieu*—when I saw you in the chalet kitchen, I almost went into cardiac arrest."

"So did I. Your appearance was so changed, I was terrified I'd never be able to get through to you."

His white smile turned her heart over. "You got through to me all right. I bolted up those stairs to give myself time to think, but my leg was slow to react."

"Raoul was so delighted to hear you'd fallen and couldn't go climbing."

Philippe nodded. "He's the best, but it's you I don't deserve," he muttered, kissing her fingertips. "You're going to hate me for what I'm about to tell you now, but at this point I have to get it all off my chest."

She smiled at him. "What else did you do that's so terrible?"

"I put Honore up to calling your home because I had to know how you were and what you were doing. When he found out you were in Nyon, I sent him on a mission, then blamed you for contacting him.''

Kellie lowered her mouth to his. ''I forgive you. Your machinations have only proved to me how much you love me.''

''I'm not through confessing,'' he admitted sheepishly.

''Go on,'' she urged, loving him all the more for unburdening himself.

He threaded his fingers through her caramel blond hair. ''Dr. Bruchard shouldn't have been subjected to a custody suit, not when I knew full well Jean-Luc wasn't mine.''

''How could you have known without a test?''

''I bribed one of the nurses in the pediatric ward to let me see the baby when Analise didn't know about it.''

''Oh darling,'' she half-laughed, half-cried. He answered with a rueful grin.

''I examined him carefully. He had a look of Yvette, but no traits of my family. None. Don't get me wrong. I loved Jean-Luc and would have loved him forever if he'd turned out to be my flesh and blood.

''That's when I conceived of the custody suit so I could get you to live with me. I was convinced that I had done so much damage to you in Zermatt, I might have driven you away forever. I needed a reason to keep you at my side.''

''None of it was necessary,'' she assured him. ''I was ready and willing to act on the smallest whisper of hope if it meant I could be with you again.''

''The closer the court date came, the more I panicked because I'd planned to withdraw the suit during the hearing and feared you'd run off the moment there was no more Jean-Luc.

"I thought if I could bribe you with the idea of setting up your own French restaurant, you'd have to stay with me until I could get you to fall in love with me again."

She cradled his unforgettable face in his hands. "You married a girl with an enormous hang-up. Yvette's unexpected entry forced me to examine my life and grow up to be a real woman at great cost to our marriage.

"You said something to me in the hospital I've never forgotten. You said, 'When we took our vows, we promised to love each other for better or for worse.' Then you grasped my hand and said, 'I never intended for there to be a for worse,' and I asked, 'but there is'?"

"I remember." His voice grated.

Her green eyes gazed into his. "That was a very naive question on my part. Whoever penned that original marriage vow understood there would be dark times with the good. We got a taste of those dark times one month into our marriage. Something I wasn't prepared for. But we're back together now.

"Much as we don't want to say it, much less think it, throughout our lives there will be other dark times among the joyous ones. I'm going to make you a vow that from here on out, I'll stand by you forever—because I'll love you forever," she said against his lips.

Overcome with emotion, Philippe pulled her back down to him. It wasn't until much later in the morning that they stirred.

"I have one more confession to make."

Sated temporarily by his lovemaking, she raised adoring eyes to him. "How much longer is this going to go on?" she teased.

"This is the last. I swear it."

"I believe you."

"Yesterday when you told me you were pregnant, I took off just like I did on those stairs at the chalet. It threw me to hear news that filled me with so much joy when our marriage was still in shambles. I needed time to think. By the time I reached Raoul's, I realized that running away was becoming a pattern with me. One I didn't like or admire in myself.

"After I told him we were expecting, Raoul offered me his congratulations, then sat there and looked at me like I'd lost my mind to be at his house instead of home with my adorable wife.

"It hit me then that all I ever wanted in this life was to be in your arms again. Prepared to beg and go on begging until you took me back, I shot out of the chair to hurry home to you. Before I reached the front door, Raoul caught up to me and told me he'd just been informed of a severe storm warning over our region.

"We took off together to secure our boats, then I planned to hold you captive in the tower until you would agree to be my wife again in the fullest sense of the word.

"But another nightmare awaited us when we pulled up by your car. The boat was missing. We searched the rental car and discovered the receipt on Claudine's credit card. That meant you'd gone out on the lake. I swear when I saw that waterspout—"

His whole body started shake. Kellie nestled closer in his arms to comfort him.

"If I'd lost you and the baby, I wouldn't have wanted to go on living, Kellie, and that's the truth."

"Don't think about it, Philippe. It's over. I'm just so

thankful you were at Raoul's instead of out on the highway where you might have had an accident.

"I called Claudine in desperation. She was my last hope. I was prepared to use her in any capacity to get my husband to love me again."

"What a fool I was not to get down on my knees to you when I discovered you at the chalet. Because of my inflexible pride, I've lost precious months watching our baby grow inside you. From now on I plan to take care of you, go to the doctor with you. I long to be your husband again. I've missed you, *mon amour,*" he whispered emotionally.

"Thank heaven we don't have to miss each other anymore. With our baby on the way, we need to start thinking about names. If it's a boy, I already have one picked out."

"I do, too," he murmured.

"Let's say it together and see what happens."

Philippe burst out laughing.

"On three, all right?"

"Whatever you say." He stole a kiss in a certain spot, almost causing her to forget what she was doing.

"Un, deux, trois."

"Raoul!" they both said at the same time.

Philippe nuzzled her neck. "Have you thought about a girl's name?'

"Yes, but I have this feeling we're going to have a boy."

Her comment coincided with the ringing of the phone. Her husband leaned across her to pick up the receiver.

When he said, "Hello, Claudine," Kellie whispered that she wanted to talk to his sister.

He kissed her shoulder. "We were just discussing

names for the baby. Want to put in your choice if it's a girl?'' he teased.

Whatever she said caused him to chuckle. ''Here's Kellie.'' He handed her the phone.

''Claudine?''

''Sorry if I'm interrupting your second honeymoon, but I'm not the only one over here dying to know if you two are back together again, as in officially.''

''The answer is a definite yes.''

''*Merci Dieu.* Now I can call the family. Everyone's waiting for the news. Even our intrepid Honore has been nervous.''

''You can tell our dear friends and family we've never been as happy.''

''I can hear your happiness.''

''Thank you for being my friend,'' Kellie's voice caught.

''You can show your appreciation by naming your daughter after me.''

''If we have a girl, I'm planning on it. Grandpa loved you. He'll be thrilled if he has a great-granddaughter bearing the name of his favorite French woman. He'll be even more thrilled when you phone him one day with the news that you're getting married.''

''I don't think that's going to happen, but we'll discuss it on another day when my brother isn't panting to get you all to himself. Which will probably be never,'' she added.

Heat swept over Kellie's body.

Philippe noticed at once and took the receiver from her. ''This conversation has been enchanting, dear sister. Speak to you again soon.''

He put the phone back on the hook, then smoothed the hair from Kellie's brow.

"What did she say to make you blush like that?"

"Oh, the kinds of things sisters say who know their brothers very very well."

"Are you going to tell me?"

"No."

"You want to make a bet?"

"No."

His smile was as exciting as it was wicked. "Because you know you're going to lose."

"I think it's time I made you breakfast, or maybe it's lunch." She tried to get out of bed but he was too quick for her.

"Not so fast, *mon amour,*" he murmured against the back of her neck. "You're going to have to stay in this bed until I get an answer out of you."

That's what she was hoping he'd say. "Then we'll be here a long, long time."

He turned her in his arms, crying her name softly before possessing her once more.

EPILOGUE

"MADAME DIDIER? Let's get one photo of you alone on the grass with your son. Then we'll be through."

"This royal photo shoot is getting to be a royal pain," Philippe whispered in her ear. He bit her lobe gently before getting up to join Lee and Raoul standing a few yards away out of range of the camera.

The prince was holding golden-haired Christine, named after Lee's mother. Their beautiful daughter, born one month after baby Raoul, had been a perfect little princess throughout the picture taking.

Kellie wished she could say the same about Raoul whose angelic black curls were deceiving. In reality he had a fun loving, adventurous nature and displayed a strong will of his own, just like someone else she knew.

Today little Raoul wasn't in the mood to have his picture taken, again reminding Kellie of someone else she knew. Talk about the acorn not falling far from the old oak tree...

"I think I want you kneeling, *madame.* We'll have you stand your son next to you."

"Come on, Raoul, sweetie. Show everybody how well you can balance."

He thought they were playing a game. As soon as she stood him up, he would sit down and laugh. Their thirteen-month-old had inherited Philippe's long, lean build and was as playful as his father.

The next time she tried to get him to remain standing,

he started falling forward into her lap. Everyone laughed except for the photographer.

"Shall we try that one more time?"

Kellie had an idea the man was losing patience in the hot summer sun. She forced Raoul to stand and look at the camera, but he decided to swing backwards and fall. At this point Philippe walked over and hunkered down a few feet away from them.

His dark eyes gleamed with amusement as he and Kellie shared a private moment. "Raoul? Come to Papa."

Like magic, his father's voice caught Raoul's attention. His green eyes lit up to see his daddy. He got to his feet and toddled toward him.

The photographer nodded. "I got a nice shot. That should do it."

"Thank goodness," Kellie muttered to Lee before they both burst out laughing. While the men changed the children into their bathing suits, Kellie followed Lee to the table and chairs set beneath the trees on the east lawn of the Château D'Arillac. It was much cooler there.

After they sat down, Lee poured them some icy cold lemonade. Kellie drank half a glass without taking a breath.

"Oh that tastes good."

"It does." Lee was already pouring herself a second round.

A new little plastic swimming pool had been filled with water. By now the sun should have warmed it. Like Lee, Kellie couldn't wait to see how the children would react. She'd brought a pocket camera, ready to take pictures for their baby book.

Pretty soon Raoul and Philippe walked them over to

the pool and carefully lowered them in the water. Christine didn't like it one bit. She started to fuss and held up her hands to get out. Her daddy pulled her back on the grass and let her walk around the pool, holding on to the rim.

Raoul, of course, was just the opposite. He plopped right down in the middle of the water and began to play with some toys.

It really was funny to watch. The men must have thought so, too. They both started to chuckle. Pretty soon they came over to the table and sat down to have some punch.

After a few minutes Christine tried to lift her leg over the side of the pool. It looked like she'd decided to get in. But she couldn't quite make it. Her lower lip wobbled and she began to cry.

With a broad smile on his face, Raoul hurried over to her and put her in the water next to his namesake. At first she stood up and looked around, then sat down. Pretty soon she wanted the toy Raoul was playing with.

Kellie was curious to see what her son would do.

He was a natural born tease. She would reach for the plastic doughnut, but he'd hold it just a mere inch away from her outstretched fingers. Growing bolder, she stood up and held on to his shoulder to get it.

When she finally took it from him, Kellie thought he'd cry. But he didn't. Instead he looked around the pool and handed her another toy. Soon she had one in each hand.

After a while she sat down and handed them back to him. They traded back and forth. They were both smiling and laughing.

"Is anyone thinking what I'm thinking?" Kellie spoke up.

Raoul's flame-blue gaze sought out Philippe's. "There will be no betrothals while I'm alive. If the two of them get together one day, it will be because they're madly in love and can't live without each other."

"Amen," Kellie's husband murmured with intense emotion.

"I don't know," Lee said with a mysterious smile on her face. "Little Raoul is our godchild. He comes from the best stock around. He's going to grow up to be as gorgeous as his father. I kind of like the idea of our daughter getting involved with him."

Playing along Kellie said, "So do I. You can see that our godchild Christine is a real charmer. A royal beauty just like her mother. She and Raoul look quite perfect together. He certainly couldn't do better than to marry a princess."

Raoul's face went chalk white. Philippe's complexion wasn't that much different.

"Darling— I was only teasing," Lee rushed to assure her husband. The anxiety in her eyes made Kellie feel guilty.

"We both were teasing," she insisted.

Raoul's reaction gave Kellie her first inkling of how traumatic it had been for him to grow up being betrothed to a woman he didn't love. Philippe had been Raoul's confidant all those years. She would never touch on the subject again.

"I'm sorry if I upset you, Raoul."

"You didn't. If I reacted, it was because this day has been magical for me." He grasped his wife's hand and clung. "I'm with the woman I love. I have a daughter I adore, and our best friends are celebrating with us.

"Your comment reminded me of all I would have missed if Philippe hadn't sat with me in my boat one hellish morning. He came up with a master plan to help break that damned betrothal. You were inspired that day, Philippe.''

Kellie's husband put his arm around her shoulders. ''That's because I'd already met my wife-to-be. I couldn't imagine being forced to marry someone I didn't love, and didn't want that to be your fate.''

She bowed her head. Once upon a time she'd thought she could force Philippe to marry Yvette. How little she'd understood of life. How much more she understood now.

Later in the day, after they'd gone home to put Raoul down for a nap, Kellie wrapped her arms around her husband.

''I love you so much, I can't fathom not being married to you.''

He sucked in his breath. ''I think maybe you're beginning to understand how I've always felt about you. Come on. Let's take our own nap.

''After today's experience I'm thinking we ought to talk about providing a little brother or sister for Raoul so he won't always want to play with Christine.''

Kellie was way ahead of him, but she kept silent as they walked through the connecting door to their bedroom. She hadn't thought the better times of their marriage could get any better, but she was wrong.

WHITE WEDDINGS

Their Big Day...
and first night!

The church is booked, the flowers are arranged, the dress is ready.... But the blushing bride and groom haven't yet stepped beyond the bedroom door!

Find out why very modern brides still wear white on their Big Day, in our brand-new miniseries in

Harlequin Romance®

starting with:

REBECCA WINTERS:
The Bridegroom's Vow
(March 2002, #3693)

BETTY NEELS:
Emma's Wedding
(May 2002, #3699)

And you're invited to two more wonderful white weddings later in 2002 from award-winning authors

LUCY GORDON and RENEE ROSZEL

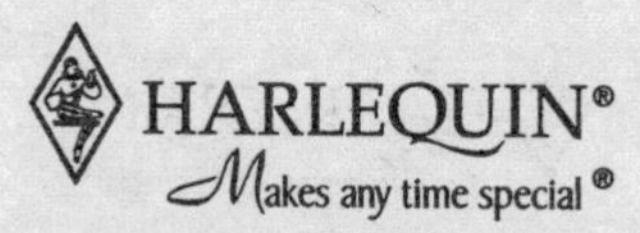

Visit us at www.eHarlequin.com

HRWW